A VAMPIRE'S FATE

FATE'S CHRONICLES
BOOK 1

RHIANNON FUTCH

CONTENTS

Prologue 1
Chapter 1 5
Chapter 2 9
Chapter 3 12
Chapter 4 17
Chapter 5 19
Chapter 6 28
Chapter 7 37
Chapter 8 45
Chapter 9 52
Chapter 10 58
Chapter 11 66
Chapter 12 74
Chapter 13 83
Chapter 14 92
Chapter 15 107
Chapter 16 120
Chapter 17 129
Chapter 18 136
Chapter 19 151
Chapter 20 159
Chapter 21 165
Chapter 22 170
Chapter 23 173

About the Author 179
Also by Rhiannon Futch 181

PROLOGUE

1833

Gretchen scans the crowd at the market. She knows her husband is deep in debt again, but sometimes the creditors will pass her by without harassment if she has Charles and his friend Devon with her. It has worked before. But even still she watches the crowd as she waits her turn with the vendor. These street markets were good for cheap food but bad for staying out of sight. Everyone comes here.

She sees them off in the distance at the same time as they notice her. She turns to the boys, "Come along, the line is mad today. We should just go." She sets a quick pace and the boys have to jog a bit to catch up to her. Charles complains that father will be mad if they come home without the meat they had been sent to bring back. Gretchen looks over her shoulder and sees the man near running at her, knife in hand. Shoving the boys out of the way, she turns back just in time to meet his eyes as he buries the blade deep in her body. "Aaaa—"

He lets her fall as he pulls the knife out of her body and walks on like nothing happened. The ground is cold under her body and the boys are kneeling over her. Charles is crying, Devon runs off for help. There is no help for her, she can feel the icy fingers of death caressing her soul. She tells Charles, "Tis his fault Charles, stay away from him, don't go home."

By the time Devon arrives with help, it is too late. Gretchen's soul watches as they close her eyes and try to console her boy. Devon puts a hand on Charles and Gretchen watches in horror as Charles accuses him of being the reason she died. She screams at them, "No, Charles! It's yer father! Stay away from yer father!" She feels an icy hand on her arm. Silent now, she turns to see Death standing next to her. "They can't hear you. They can't see you. I am so sorry." She wants to cry at the unfairness of it.

Judson's fault! All of it! Should be him here, dead in the square. Death touches her arm again, "It is time, we must go."

She looks one last time at her son, "Will it be different next time?"

Death smiles sadly, "It isn't likely."

As SEEN by Mary the seer when visited by Fate and Prudence in October of the year 2000.

1

Quick note: If you enjoy A Vampire's Fate, be sure to check out my offer of a free Fate's Chronicles novella at the end. Happy reading!

The funeral went on forever. It was all I could do to stay calm while the pastor read off trite crap for the mourners. Now that they're gone I can tell Charlie how I really feel.

"Damn you for dying, you bastard. I know your mom would say I shouldn't talk ill of the dead, but who gives a rat's ass what she thinks today? Not me. How could you leave me like this? We're supposed to grow old together, you fucker. I am only 40! THAT. IS. NOT. OLD. You weren't old either! 41 is not old and you should still be here. With me." I shove my knuckle in my mouth to stop the sob that wants to break free, "How could you leave me like this Charlie? Fuck you for eating all that crap while I begged you to eat better. Fuck you for refusing to exercise. Fuck you for ignoring me and the doctor. How do I live without you asshole? Answer me that? How the fuck am I supposed to go on without you in my life?" The tears flow from my eyes and I let them go unchecked. Who's going to say anything to the widow about her makeup running down her face?

Nobody with a brain in their head, Prudence would slap them silly. I glance over at Prudence, waiting with our friends by the limo. They all look worried about me. I guess I can't blame them. I would worry about them if they were standing by a dead husband's grave telling him off and crying. My black dress hides the tears that fall on it, mostly. Someone told me I look 'too Morticia' in this dress today. I told them to go fuck themselves right as Prudence hauled them off for a talk. My sister really is the best in so many ways.

As for the dress, it is Charlie's favorite. I probably won't wear it again after today since he won't be there to whistle at me and say crude things. "Fuck you for leaving me, Charlie. You were supposed to stick around and keep me from being alone, that was your whole damn job. I have to go now, there'r assholes waiting to gather in our house and eat food. I'll come see you real soon." It takes a few more minutes for me to leave him there in the ground. I eventually muster up the willpower to turn myself away from his grave and walk toward my friends.

THIS RECEPTION BLOWS. His parents have made it all about them and that would be fine except everyone feels bad for me now and they all feel the need to come talk about it. I don't want to talk about it. I don't want to talk. I want them all to go away and leave me to wallow in my misery. Natasha, Memré and Prudence have been great about steering people away from me but more just take their place. Prudence wanders back over, Charlie's boss Steve now steered over to and talking with three other coworkers.

She asks me if I am okay. I laugh and am shocked at the harsh sound that comes from my mouth. Serious now, I tell her, "No. I'm not ok. I hate having all these damn people here in my house and his parents haven't been here in years till today but they are acting like it is their place. I just want to chill out. Maybe get really drunk. I can't deal with these people." Prudence nods, her lips compressed into a thin line, "Then they are all going to leave. Go hide in your bedroom sis, lock the damn door." With that she marches off to battle, collecting Natasha and Memré on the way.

I make my way through the house to our bedroom, stepping into the blissful silence, I shut and lock the door behind me. I don't even make it to the bed to sit down before I hear my mother-in-law, Jacki, at the door. It sounds like she is angry about having her petty show disrupted. I don't care. I strip off the funeral clothing, laying the dress he loved carefully over a chair. Stepping into the closet, I grab some sweats and a tee. I need the comfort right now.

Jackie has moved away from the door. It sounds like they sent Natasha to fetch her. Sweats on, I pull the tee over my head. Jackie tried to corner me earlier and feed me some line about Charlie wanted them to have the house. Right after she did that, I emailed our lawyer Benjamin. He sent back that Charlie had warned him about them when we were doing our wills. He also mentioned that Charlie had made sure his parents could take nothing from me.

Charlie had been visiting with Benjamin every six months to keep his will up to date. And he made videos for me. I can't watch those today, but I will. Soon. I lay on his side of the bed so I can smell him. How can he be gone? I hear a knock at my door and Memré says, "It's safe now. You can come out. We're making drinks." I tell her I will be right out and I bury my face in his pillow one more time, a last deep inhale before I get up and go join them.

2

"It's been nearly a year since he died Fate. You need to get out of the house, have some fun. It doesn't have to be serious." Memré stops her diatribe to sip her tea. I pull my knees up to my chest in the chair and stare out the window as I sip my coffee. Unlike Memré, whose day is near over, mine begins as the sun goes down.

Once Charlie left I lost interest in facing mornings, so I talked to the university and got my shifts changed to nights. My new boss Natasha has also been my friend and coven sister for years. Memré has been my friend and coven sister for even longer. Right now I am sick of both of them. They mean well, but I can't go through losing someone I love again.

Especially when it was so preventable. After the autopsy the doctor said that it was surprising he had lived this long with all the stuff in his arteries. Memré is clearing her throat rather loudly. I look over at her and raise an eyebrow, "Are you done with your speech?" She narrows her eyes at me and turns her face away from me. I relent, "Ok. I'm sorry. I'm not ready to go out. If I ever get ready, I will absolutely come to you first. For now, the idea of dating someone is repugnant. Please, please understand. When it happens, I won't fight it. Until then, let's just let this dead horse lie? Please?"

Memré gives me a sad smile, "Of course. I'll let it go. I just want to see you happy. If the single life is what makes you happy right now, well, I would be a hypocrite to say no. It isn't like I have been overly eager to seek my own fun since I helped put Shelton in prison." She reaches over and takes my hand, "You know I love you. I hurt seeing you so lonely." I squeeze her hand lightly, "I do. I love you too. And now, I have to get ready for work. The library really frowns on the wearing of fuzzy pajamas by its employees."

Memré laughs at my joke and takes her cup to the kitchen. I stand and walk with her to the door where she reminds me to lock it after she leaves. Closing and locking the door behind her, I chuckle. They seem to have the idea that since Charlie died, I must be completely reckless. I glance at my watch, crap. I have to get going soon. Setting my cup on the table as I pass, I head into my bedroom to get ready for another night at the library. One white button-up shirt, a pair of black slacks, and my flats have me dressed.

I look around for the glasses I was wearing before I

changed clothes, I don't see them anywhere. Bah. I head to the bathroom and pull the magnifying mirror toward me. As I do, I spot a pair of my glasses resting on the cotton ball container. I have no idea why I put them there, but I am quite sure I did. I check my watch, shit. If I don't get out of here quickly, I won't have time to stop and see Charlie. I throw some mascara on and gloss my lips. I am not there to impress anyone, anyway. That done, I grab my purse as I run out the door and then right back to lock it. Maybe Memré was right to worry about me...

3

I park as close to Charlie's grave as I can. Hustling as I have only a few minutes today. My friends and my sister don't know that I come here to talk to him every day. I just need to talk to him still. We were together for years and we spoke every day.

Well, he did most of the talking when he was alive and it left me with a lot to say to him. I don't know how to not talk to him every day. Maybe one day I will figure it out, but today is not that day. I tell him I can't stay long today because I spent too long convincing Memré that I don't need to date.

I swear I can hear his laughter in the wind. I pick up the flower I left yesterday and replace it with a fresh one from our garden. Blowing a kiss at him, I go back to the car and start the drive to work.

I ARRIVE AT WORK, just making it in on time. The stack of books that need checked in and shelved is daunting to say the least. I jump right into it as it makes the night fly when I stay busy. Natasha comes in looking gorgeous as always. She has this glorious hourglass figure that she accents well with form fitting skirts in inky colors and jewel tone shirts. Today is a dark blue skirt with a royal blue shirt that fits her perfectly and looks comfortable too.

I do not envy her nude pumps, those things are not for me. I greet her as I continue to check books in; she says hi and steps into her office. Coming back out, the files she carried are gone. She comes over to stand on the opposite side of the bin I am working to unload and begins to hand me books. She works with me in silence for a time. But like all good things, that comes to an end as she starts to speak.

"Sooo, I was thinking." I stop and look at her, brows raised. She continues, "I thought it might be time for you to start getting out there. You're way too young to just close up shop." I shake my head, "Oh good grief. Not you too? I don't want to date. I don't want to get out there, wherever there is. I am not ready for that and I don't know if I will ever be ready. Can we please just let it go at I will get out there as soon as I am ready?"

Natasha frowns but nods in agreement, "Yeah. I will let it go. Maybe you could come out with me a little more? We could have breakfast soon," she throws her empty hands up, palms out, "just you and I. No dates, no men. Once a week? And I promise not to ask again."

I smile at my friend, "It's a deal. Breakfast out once a week with you and no more get out there conversations." She nods in approval, "Good then. Now, I have all the paperwork to tend to, so I will leave you to your cart." She walks off to her office and closes the door behind her. I continue checking books in and stacking them on the cart next to me.

I realize I have been staring about the time he realizes he has been staring as well. I welcome him to the library and quickly move my eyes down, away from his face. Only to notice the swell at the juncture of his god-like thighs. Crap. I can feel the blush starting, I am too pale to be able to hide this at all. I tip my head so my hair falls forward on either side of my face, effectively screening my blush.

Of course now is when I am all thumbs and manage to drop a book I was trying to check in. I kneel down to pick it up and as I straighten I realize he is standing just in front of my section of the help desk. Dammit. Now I have to help him. Oh good, looks like he is blushing too. "Hi, what can I help you with this evening?" I ask, putting aside the book I just fetched from the floor.

"Hi, I am Devon. And you are?" He puts his hand out toward me to shake and complete the introduction, but I am still stuck on his voice. It sent shivers to places that need to mind their business.

I finally recall how to human and shake his hand

quickly as I tell him, "Fate. My name is Fate. Is there something I can do for you Devon?" He smiles at me and now my panties are wet. For fuck's sake. I haven't had this reaction in years, I am too old for this nonsense.

"Yes you can. I need help finding some research materials and I am unfamiliar with your system. Perhaps you could assist me?" A shiver runs through my body as all the ways I would like to assist him run through my mind. I give myself a mental shake and agree to give him a quick lesson on our databases. It is part of my job. I ask to see his library membership or university id before we head over to a seating area. At least now I will know his name and maybe in the future I can avoid him, like the plague.

I don't need anything resembling a possible relationship, I have plenty of toys thank you very much. He hands over his membership card, so not a student or a professor, good. Devon Kordell, interesting name.

I scan it just in case maybe I can tell him to leave because the card is a fake. Sadly, it comes up valid. I hand him back his card and walk around, exiting the back area through the door at the other end of the counter.

I lead him to a desk as far away from the counter I have been working at the past few hours as is possible. He sits and I pull up a nearby chair to sit and wait while he sets up his laptop. I can't believe I am having such a reaction to this guy.

I can almost feel a magnet in him pulling at all the parts on me that are now begging to be touched. The thought makes me even more angry at him for being so damn delectable. I hear him clear his throat and I look over at him. He says, "Hey, Earth to Fate. Ready?"

I blush. Again, dammit. What is wrong with me? "Yes, yes, let's get this over with." I quickly run him through a nice simple tutorial which he completely fucks up by asking all these reasonable, well thought out questions. I hate him. And I want to jump his bones.

Oh Sweet Lady, I need help. I answer all his questions and help him find some papers to aid in his research on vampires. Weird, but whatever. I just want to get away from him. Or climb in his lap. I accidentally roll my eyes out loud and he raises an eyebrow at me. I raise an eyebrow back at him before telling him, "I think you are all set now, Mr. Kordell. You—"

He interrupts to say, "Please, call me Devon." I nod, "Ok, Devon, you should be all set. I will be at the front desk if you need further help." I stand, grabbing my chair and sliding it back to where it belongs before I all but run back to the front desk.

4

Fate is running away from me. I wonder how many other people can say their Fate ran away from them? I am so glad she doesn't seem to have noticed that nothing in my pants is behaving. Now that she is gone I shift to ease some of the pressure in there.

Her name is perfect for her. Does she like her name? Will she still love me? Will she choose to walk away from the bond we have? What do I do if she does? I have to talk to Billy. I know she and I are meant for each other.

If Charles tries to kill her again, I don't think I can stop myself from killing him. What if all the old tales are true? What if I kill my maker and that kills me too? I would leave her alone to suffer like I have every time she was taken from me. I open a chat window in my computer and send a message to Billy. Hopefully, he is available wherever he is...

Devon: Billy, I found her. She is here in North Carolina. Charles has shown up within days every time I find her. I can't lose her again. Please, come help me protect her.:

Billy: I keep tellin' you, it's your emotions that gives it away to him. Will try to rouse the twins. It will be a bit before I can get there, I am right in the middle of a situation here. Be there as soon as I can.:

Devon: Where are the twins at these days? I haven't heard from anyone recently.:

Billy: That's because you go into feckin hiding every month and it's a gawddamn beast tryin' to get in touch. Stop changing your feckin number, asshole.:

Devon: Erm, sure thing. See you soon. Keep in touch then.:

Billy: I will. And I will get there as soon as I can get myself extricated from the current situation. You can keep her safe until then. You are much stronger than he is for all that he was your maker.:

That is exactly what worries me.

I stare at the blinking cursor a moment more before I close the chat and start actually reading some of the papers we pulled up. Perhaps one of them will have the answers that I seek.

5

"Charlie, you are not going to believe this shit." He doesn't answer me out loud anymore, but I can almost see him raise his eyebrows at me and ask me what he isn't going to believe. I am sitting on his grave. People give me looks, but I don't care. He would have wanted me as close as possible.

I continue on, "Yesterday all anyone could talk to me about was moving on. Going out. Having some fun. And I really wanted nothing to do with it. Then last night this guy comes in and Charlie, I wanted to take him right there. I know you won't have any problems hearing about this since you hadn't wanted to have sex with me for a really long time before you died anyway. So I feel like the least you could do is listen to me now. I couldn't stop thinking about him last night. I killed the batteries in my vibrator. Which, to be fair, had been in there a long time."

I shake my head, "That isn't the point though. The

point is, I think there must be something wrong with me. Why else would I see a stranger and suddenly feel like we have been connected forever?" I sit there in silence with Charlie for a little while longer. The peace I usually feel isn't really here today, but I stubbornly sit there in the belief that it will arrive.

The time for me to go if I plan to arrive at work on time draws closer and I stand, telling my Charlie goodbye and that I will come visit him again tomorrow. I turn to leave and I see some blond hunk of a man across the cemetery at a different gravesite. He smiles and waves, I return the gesture and head to my car.

THE LIBRARY HAS BEEN PACKED this evening; I wonder what professor assigned a paper? The students have all been looking for books on various famous figures. It's all been biographies today and thank goddess we have multiple copies of the more popular books right now. Things have finally slowed down now that it is after ten.

I am behind on the re-shelving so I grab a cart and start to check in books. I freeze in place as I see the gorgeous blond man from the cemetery walk into my library. What are the chances of that happening? He sees me and smiles; I blush and smile back. Where is all this male attention coming from? Why are they suddenly noticing a 40-year-old librarian? Did Charlie's death have some weird effect on me that made me more attractive?

Ugh. I need to do some research of my own, of the witchy kind. I don't think it is possible, but weird things happen when magic is involved.

The blond stranger is heading toward me. Admittedly, that is less strange than his being here since I am behind the desk. "Hello, can I help you?" I ask with my best customer service voice. He manages to smile even bigger, like he recognizes the voice. "Yes, you can help me Mrs?" I blink, wow, that voice. He sounds like I would think a Greek God would have sounded like. "Owens, Ms. Owens. What can I do for you?" I decline to ask his name, the guy seems really nice, and he is definitely good looking in the conventional way, but my witchy senses are tingling.

His eyes narrow so slightly I almost think I imagined it. But I know I didn't. Forty years on this planet have taught me to listen to my intuition. "Why Ms. Owens, you wound me. It would seem almost as though you aren't interested in knowing my name." He flashes me a smile as he grabs at his chest like his heart is breaking. I smile at him, going along just to get him to the point already. I have a ton of books to check in.

Satisfied with my participation he continues, "I have a research project starting very soon and I have requested the university allow me to utilize one of the rooms here in the library as I will be relying heavily on the resources available here. They have granted me a room," he waves toward the back where there are some locked rooms made available for visiting researchers, "back there.

Sadly, my assistant has just taken an extended leave of absence. Now I have no help. Would it be possible to enlist your aid when you are not otherwise occupied?" The balls on this guy. I manage to keep a smile pasted on my face, but barely. "I'm sorry, I am not available for research projects. However, if you speak to the university, I am sure they will be happy to assist you with an intern or two."

Touché ballsy.

He frowns, bringing a hand to his chin with the other crossed in front of him to cup his elbow. Tapping his chin with a finger he seems to be thinking, I have my doubts. "Hmm, that might work. But I really would prefer someone more mature like yourself. I really dislike the chatter of children." Closing my eyes in frustration, I take a deep calming breath.

He smells nice, at least. "Well, we have students of all ages here so you should have no problems there. Just be sure to make your requirements clear to the university. They will help you however possible, I am sure. Now, if you don't need me to pull up a paper or place a book request. I haven't even seen your ID, and I don't have time to waste on people that aren't patrons of the library..." I let the sentence drift off and look toward the door, hoping he will take a hint.

No such luck.

He actually leans on the counter, "Perhaps," he reaches across the counter and takes my hand. I am so amazed at the audacity, I just stand there to see where he is taking this, "I could request you specifically from the university. I have made sizable donations, they might be willing to accommodate my wishes in this matter. They are printing my ID card right now."

He starts rubbing my hand with his thumb and I snatch it out of his, "No. As a matter of fact, they will not be accommodating you in this because I said no. N. O. Now, as I said before, I have work to do. I think you should leave and go work on getting that ID because without you don't belong in the building. Have a nice day." His smile slipped while I spoke and his face grew darker as I neared the end of my little set down.

He straightens and slams his hands on the counter, "Now you listen to me MS. OWENS." His voice rises with each word and I hear the click of Natasha's door opening, she steps out, suddenly he is all charm and smiles again.

Natasha has way too much fire in her not to feel the current in the air and she glides over exuding authority, "Are you having a problem with this gentleman Fate?" I nod, "Yes, he seems to have lost his way to the exit. He is very confused." Natasha looks at him in that cold way she has perfected, "Well, good sir, you are in luck. The door is just over there," she points at the door to the left of our desk area, "and we look forward to seeing you again when you are not feeling so very confused as to how to treat our staff. Have a nice rest of your evening, sir."

She smiles and extends her arm toward the door in a guiding motion. His face is dark again, but controlled this time as he says, "Thank you ladies, I look forward to seeing you again as I work on my project. Have a nice evening." His smile is that of an ego-driven jerk, sure that he will win us over. We watch in silence as he leaves the library.

Once the doors close completely behind him I turn to Natasha, "Thank you for having my back. That guy just feels wrong. He sets all my witchy senses off and he wanted me to be his research assistant. Yuck. No. If he does request me through the university, tell them I will quit before I will work with him." Natasha hugs me to her, "I'm so sorry I didn't get out here sooner!" She releases me and steps back, "I was knee deep in paperwork and I wasn't paying attention until he made that loud noise, what was he doing?"

I describe the whole incident to her and she shakes her head, "What a jerk. Yeah, I will talk to the university chairs myself and make sure they do not assign any women to aid him. Ridiculous behavior. Do you want me to stay out here? In case he comes back?" I think about it, looking toward the door. What if that dark guy comes back? I might could use her presence to keep my hands off of him. "No, just uh, maybe leave your door open so you can hear the sounds out here better?"

Natasha starts toward her office, "Sure thing love, and I will be paying attention too." I take a deep breath to clear my head and get back to that pile of check-ins.

It's two am when I feel him walking toward the library. It's like nothing I have ever felt before. But I know Devon Kordell is about to walk through the library doors and I can't do anything but watch for a glimpse of him. I feel like a woman starved for the touch of this one particular man. How is this even possible? I only met him yesterday!

The doors open and Devon steps into the library, his gaze zeroes in on me like he knew where I was as well. We drift toward each other, my cart of books left abandoned as I am pulled to this man. We stop an inch from each other and I breathe in his scent; he smells like patchouli and books. I could breathe him in all day. I see his nostrils flare as he drinks in my scents as well.

My eyes are drawn to his, I could fall into those eyes, deep like a black forest pond. I catch myself reaching toward his hand and I shake my head, stepping back I clear my throat. "Nice to see you, Mr. Kordell. May your research prove fruitful tonight." I turn to run back to my cart. No shame here. I hear him snort in disgust behind me and I stop.

Looking back at him, I say, "Excuse me?" He glares at me, glares! "When did you get so scared, Fate? And call me Devon. Mr. Kordell was my father, and he is long gone from this existence." I turn fully around to confront him, "I am not scared of you or anyone else, Devon Kordell. I have work to do and no desire to flaunt library policy with a passing patron." I turn and walk to my cart as he laughs at me, the jerk.

I feel him walking toward me and he stops just

behind me, not even our clothing touches as he whispers in my ear, "I would love to hear more about what you do desire, Fate." I feel a sense of loss as he walks away to seat himself and I shiver with longing. A deep breath and I shelve the books that belong in this spot before moving on.

A few books later I realize he has seated himself so that he can watch me wherever I am with few exceptions. Usually I would find that behavior creepy, but if he feels anything like I do then how the hell could I hold that against him? Especially since all I want to hold against him is me. Besides, I only noticed because I have been watching him. All I can think about is him, and his shoulders. Those thighs. Good grief, it's like being a teenager again.

I hear him chuckling and I turn to glare at him, he just smiles and asks, "Am I distracting you Fate?" His voice makes my knees weak, but he will not know that. "No. You are not distracting me, Devon. You are disturbing me in my work. You should get to yours." I make a shooing motion at him and grab another book off my cart, turning to place it in its spot.

As I turn back around to move to the next spot he is there, just a breath away, "I disturb you Fate? Hmm, I think it would be much nicer to distract you. Would you have breakfast with me when you leave here tonight?" I suck in a breath, even more turned on at his nearness, "No Devon, I will not have breakfast with you. I am not interested in having breakfast with anyone. And you especially." His face falls, he actually looks heartbroken, I can't take that.

I place a hand on his arm and I watch his eyes float closed in pleasure at my touch. I fight the same reaction in myself, the joy generated from the contact between our skin is stunning. "Wait, Devon, it isn't you. I don't want to date anyone because I am still mourning my husband. He died recently, well, nearly a year ago. I am deeply attracted to you and that terrifies me because I can't go through losing someone again. I am too broken for this, do you understand?" His eyes open and I am surprised to see a dampness at the corners of his eyes as he says, "Oh Fate, I understand so much better than you could ever imagine. I am very sorry for your loss. But love, we are meant to be together. Our names are written together in eternity. I understand if you need some time. Though I know you can feel it just as much as I do." He raises a hand and caresses my face with a feather-lite touch that feels like heaven. I feel myself leaning into his hand and I force my body to stop. He smiles sadly at me, "I will let you work now, love." He turns and walks back to his seat as my heart shatters to watch him walk away.

Oh, I am in so much trouble.

6

Oh wonderful.

Here comes Charles the creepy. Just the same as every night for the past week. Charles arrives in the early evening, pretends to work while following me around and then leaves around midnight. Just when I think I might get some work done, in walks Devon and all I can focus on is him and his package.

Maybe if I look especially busy with this paperwork, Charles will leave me alone tonight. Or maybe ducks will fly out of my ass and start granting wishes for the patrons. Futile as it may be I act like I don't see Charles as he heads toward the desk I am sitting behind.

I REALLY AM WORKING, but definitely able to split my attention if I wanted to do so. Charles stops in front of the desk and I just continue to ignore him until he clears his throat. I look up, he smiles and holds out a gift-wrapped box, "I brought you a gift." I smile weakly and take the box from him, "Um, thanks. Why are you bringing me a gift? I don't think you should be giving me gifts. You should take this back, I can't accept this." I try to hand it back to him but he steps back out of reach, holding his hands up with the palms facing me.

"No Fate, it is a gift. It will upset me greatly if you don't accept my gift. It is simply a token of my appreciation for your lovely company this past week." My jaw drops open as he speaks, lovely company? I told him to go away at least once every evening. "I think maybe you have me confused with someone else? I have been telling you to go away all week. It was just last night I told you I would rather sit in a fire than talk to you again. Are you feeling ok? Do you need a doctor? I think maybe you are having a stroke."

He laughs and I am really concerned that this guy is delusional.

Then he starts talking and confirms his delusional state, "Yes you have, and it has been the best thing. I have never met a woman quite like you, Fate. Most women chase after me and throw themselves at me. Now that I find myself in a similar position, I understand the thrill of the hunt." A predatory gleam crosses his face and is quickly hidden.

I just shake my head, "Oh, are you barking up the wrong tree. Look, Mr. Armstrong, I am unequivocally interested in being nearly anything but yours. We are never going to be an item, I will not date you. If you insist that I keep this gift, so be it. It does not mean I owe you anything. It does not mean we are together in any way. Now go away so I can finish my work."

The jerk just grins even wider, "I love it when you speak so definitively Fate. I bet you are a real firecracker in bed." He turns and saunters off toward his research room in the back of the library. Ugh, so creepy. I look at the box in my hand. I don't like it, it looks like a ring box. I lift the lid.

It fucking well is an engagement ring.

Dammit.

He brought me a gorgeous ring with an enormous emerald cut sapphire surrounded by small diamonds with more diamonds on the band to either side of the stone. This looks like a really expensive engagement ring. What is wrong with this guy? I have told him every way I know how to that I am not even thinking about being interested in him. Whatever. I set the box down on my desk and continue on with my work. Maybe his lunacy will stay in his research room tonight until it is time for him to leave.

AH YES, nearly two am and I can feel Devon draw closer to the library. He really is funny and sweet and the most sexy man I have ever met. If I wasn't so terrified that I wouldn't be able to live through another loss, I would have sex with him in an instant. It couldn't be just sex with him though, if it was just sex I wouldn't feel him walking up the sidewalk.

I wouldn't know the instant he walked through the door. My eyes wouldn't seek him like I am starved for the sight of him though I see him every night I work here. He really is stunning. His head is turning toward me as he walks through the door. A smile lights up his face as he walks toward me and damned if I can do anything but smile back at him.

He stops in front of me, in the same place Charles stood earlier this evening. "Hello beautiful, how are you this evening? Any closer to having breakfast with me?" I laugh, "I might, if only I wasn't sure you would break my heart, you charmer." He grins, "Oh darlin', I would never do such a thing. You wound me to the core. Say you'll have breakfast with me so my heart might keep beating a little longer." He slumps dramatically over the counter as I laugh at him. "Get up, silly man. People are starting to stare." I stand and lightly shove at those gorgeous shoulders, not that I expect them to move unless he decides to do so.

He laughs and straightens, "I suppose I can go on since you laid your sweet hands on me." He spots the box on my desk and pointing toward it he says, "You have another admirer?" I scowl at the box as though it were Charles sitting there. "Yes. Unfortunately, I do. He isn't near so pleasant as you, but he is here doing research and following me around early every evening. I've told him every way I can think of to go away, but he just won't. Tonight he brought this," I pick up the box and hand it to Devon, "as a token of his appreciation for my company this week. He said he would be upset if I didn't accept it. I figure I can throw it in a drawer, it will make a great re-gift for someone."

As I have been talking Devon opened the box and frowned at the ring inside, "Fate, this is an engagement ring." He looks at me, his brows drawn low over his eyes. "Would you be mad if I started coming by earlier in the evening for your safety? It worries me that you have been telling him to go away and tonight he brought you an engagement ring. He sounds dangerous for you." I nibble on my lip, "I don't know Devon. I agree that he is possibly dangerous, but spending more time with you is dangerous for me as well."

He smiles softly at me, "Sweet Fate, are you a witch in this life too?" My eyes open wide at that and I look around quickly to see if anyone is close enough to hear him before hissing, "How do you know about that? Shhhh! Don't say anything right now. We can't talk about this here, someone might hear us. The answer is yes, but for now just hush and go sit. Do your research." He cocks an eyebrow at me, "I will go sit for now. But I will be escorting you to your car this morning and we will talk then." He hands the ring back to me and turns on his heel to take his usual seat in the middle where he can see everything.

I sigh, I am in so much trouble. Setting the ring down, I get back to work.

    🐦

EIGHT AM HAS NEVER SEEMED to take so long to arrive. But now that it has, I am apprehensive about walking out to the car with Devon. I don't fear him at all. It's me I fear, my reactions to him. But if he wants to talk about things like witchcraft, we can't do that in the library. I clock out and exit the desk area, Devon is waiting by the doors.

I wonder how he knows when I get off work? He isn't usually here when I leave. I stop a little away from him, "I haven't agreed to go to breakfast with you, only to talk with you outside the library. Are we clear about that?" Devon nods, "Yes Fate, you are crystal clear, and that is why I worry about your admirer. I know you want me and yet you are very vocal in maintaining a distance for your own good. How vocal must you be when you actually want someone to go away?" He steps through the door pushing it open with his free hand and turning to hold it open for me, "Shall we dear lady?"

I blush and walk through the doorway, ambling toward my car. He falls in step with me before I am two steps from the doorway. He is amazingly fast. We walk in silence to my car. Once there, he asks if I will wait long enough for him to put his things in his car and return. He points to a car a few rows over. "Sure, no problem. Go on, I will stow my things while you do. I won't even drive off while your back is turned." He grins and heads off toward his car.

I unlock mine and lean in to set my purse and book on the passenger seat. As I lean back out, a hand grabs my arm and slams me against the open door before slinging me over to slam against the car. Before I can summon air to do my bidding I feel the hand on my upper arm ripped away and I hear a body hitting the pavement and… growls?

I hear growling.

I slowly turn and see Devon restraining a very pale mugger. I don't think the guy is usually so pale, but he looks terrified. That might have something to do with it. I think Devon is growling at him. I reach down slowly, I feel a little dazed, to touch Devon's shoulder. I don't know why I feel the need to touch him but it seems the right, the only thing I can do. He jumps when my hand rests on his shoulder and he turns his head to look at me. His eyes look strange, but it doesn't matter as much as the ground rushing up at me.

I wake up laying on the pavement, my head is pounding like a drum set with an exuberant five-year-old behind the wheel. Devon's face is hovering above me. "Fate, can you hear me? Fate? Are you back with me yet?" I start to nod and think better of that idea, "Yes. My head hurts like the devil, but I am here, not so bloody loud. What happened?

Last thing I remember is touching your shoulder and the pavement rushing up at me." He chuckles, "Ah, the pavement didn't move but you definitely did. I had subdued your attacker but when you touched my shoulder and started falling I had to catch you. Don't worry though, he is taken care of and won't bother you again." There is an odd note in his voice, something tells me I shouldn't ask but, "What do you mean taken care of?"

He glances away, "Let's not worry about that right now, hmm? How about we get you up off this pavement and home?" Now I feel a little panicked, I can't drive home. Not like this. I must have made a noise or a face because Devon answers, "Don't worry, love, I will drive you home." He moves away from me briefly, I hear some things move and my doors lock before he shuts my car door. "How are you going to get me home without my car?" He chuckles, "Oh yeah, you are definitely not driving anywhere. We are taking my car Fate. Does your phone know where you live?"

He lifts me so gently it almost doesn't make my head throb a little more. Wow, is he strong. He isn't even breathing hard. We arrive at another vehicle and he opens a door, slowly lowering my feet to touch the ground and easing me into a seat. He pushes a button and the seat smoothly lays back, as it stops moving he lifts my legs to set them into the car.

"Fate, love, does your phone know where you live?" I chuckle, "What a strange question. Unthinkable the first time I was born. I know where I live, I cannot speak for my phone good sir." I hear Devon exhale, he takes my hand, so weird. Then he places my thumb on a flat surface. I would probably recognize it if I opened my eyes. But there are so many strange memories floating in my mind right now, I can't seem to focus on the things outside of my head.

7

"This is a very nice car. Are you laughing at me? I feel like you're laughing at me. You wouldn't laugh if I did that thing I used to do that you liked so much. Do you remember that? It was when we lived in England. What year was it..." He answers my question, "It was 1856. I'm a little surprised that you remember it."

I nod, not the smartest thing I have done recently. "OOOOOWWW. Yes, I seem to be recalling a great many things now that my brain is working so diligently to escape the confines of my skull. I recall that we have had a loooot of sex and it was very enjoyable. I think I would like to do that again. It has been a year, give or take a little, since Charlie passed away. Did you know I am still mad at him for that? I told him off at his funeral. I still miss him. He was my friend, not so much my lover as we got older, but he was my friend and I miss my friend." My traitorous eyes leak again, as they do every time I say Charlie's name.

Good thing they are closed so I can't tell if he is seeing this or not. "I missed you too. Every time I died and had to go away, I was so sad to leave you. Did you find the person that kept killing me? Are they like you? You look the same every time I come back. How are you doing that? Do you request a specific body type every time? I think I would like to keep this one. This is a good body. This is the longest I have gotten to keep a body, isn't it? Maybe that's why I like it so much, it's the one I have known the longest."

The car stops and he asks me, "Do you want me to respond to any of that or is it a stream of consciousness and I should just listen in silent amusement?" I stick my tongue out in his general direction, one of the few things I can do without causing explosions in my head, "Yes, I would like answers, and a lot less sass from you, mister. Or that tongue thing is definitely not happening."

He chuckles again, "In the order you asked then, Yes, I was laughing at you. Yes, I remember the thing you did, though I feel like I already answered that one by responding with a year. No, I was not aware that you were still mad at your husband for dying. I am sorry for your loss and I am sorry that you felt the loss of me each time. I do know who has been killing you. Yes, in fact, they are like me." He pulls the car into my driveway, puts it in park, and continues, "The rest of your questions will have to wait. We need to get you in your house and get you some aspirin, maybe some tea. Do you like tea?"

I manage to stop myself before I nod, "I do like tea. I like tea much better than aspirin. I have some tea with willow bark, black tea leaves, and hibiscus. It tastes much better than those pills go down and I would rather have that." He nods, grabs my purse out of the back of the car and appears next to my door.

He has it open before I have even summoned the energy to summon the will to lift my head. It feels so full. He helps me out of the car and even as gentle as we go my head is pounding. "What— what kind of car is this, anyway? Looks fancy." He is silent as we float to the door, or maybe I am the one floating? "Do you really want to know about my car right now?" We stop at my door and he holds my purse out in front of me, I shove my hand into the side pocket, straight to the bottom. I find my keys slightly to the left of where my hand touched the bottom, I draw them out with a triumphant cry, "Ha! Found them! And yes, talking helps to distract me from the pain in my brain. What kind of car is that?"

He takes my keys from me and quickly starts trying them till he finds the right one as he tells me, "It is an Audi A8 e. It is rather fancy though not as fancy as some others, nor is it so flashy." Opening the door he walks in and though I would swear I am walking I still feel floaty. I hear him kick the door shut and flinch at the slam, both of which make my head pound.

"Where is your kitchen? Why do you live in suburban

hell?" He scoops me up and doesn't wait for directions, but I point the general way for him. He moves so fast, it tickles my brain and I feel like there is something about that I should remember...

He sets me down slowly, and gently, then slides out a chair from my little wooden table. It is old and scarred, thousands of meals graced this table before I found it and I love it. It was one of the few things Charlie and I argued about. He wanted one of those modern glass top tables, but I hate them. I don't want to see people's feet when I look down at my table. I also didn't want anything to do with cleaning a glass table all the time.

Devon helps me ease down into the chair in a way that won't jostle my head further. He is describing his car in great detail. Silver on the outside, dark gray leather inside. Tinted windows so dark that no one can see in but he never gets pulled over, he says the car is too white for that though he thinks if they saw the darkness of his skin he would be harassed a lot.

He asks where I keep the tea as he fills the enameled kettle from the stove. "It's in the pantry, the very back. There is a light switch, just next to the door. It is in a blue glass jar and labeled headache tea. Make sure you grab the honey while you are in there, that tea needs honey. Too much bitter and tart in it, have to add some sweet or it won't be drunk. Drank? Ugh. That shit isn't going down without some sweet. I like honey." He comes back out of the pantry with the blue jar of tea and another jar with honey.

I watch as he methodically searches my kitchen, starting with the cabinets on the far side and interspersing them with the drawers. I could have told him that the cups are two cabinets away from the stove and the tea ball is in the drawer farthest from the stove and closest to me. But why ruin his fun? Or my entertainment. I should rearrange that entire kitchen.

It is all still exactly as Charlie wanted, even though he didn't cook or do anything in the kitchen beyond eat what I served him. Even the colors in the house, it is all reds and browns. I like purples and blues and greens. The kettle barely starts to whistle when he lifts it from the stove and pours the steaming liquid into the cup. He gives it a stir and brings it over to me. After he sets the cup in front of me I lift it up and blow on it to cool it. It doesn't work, but the habit of it makes me happy.

He pulls out the chair next to me and seats himself, "Would you let me cook for you?" I sip at the tea to hide my shock. Memories are surfacing of him cooking for me in past lives, but I have no experience with a man taking care of me in this life. Charlie was a good guy but I am seeing more and more that he was a lot of extra work for me. We weren't the partners I liked to say we were and that, that makes me sad that I spent so much time fooling myself.

"Yes," I say, "it would be much appreciated if you would cook for me." My voice is much smaller than I want anyone to notice, especially Devon. He eyes me but decides against asking any questions. I am very grateful for this as I watch him search my, no, Charlie's kitchen. "Are you particular to anything?" I almost laugh but I am afraid it might become tears so I just tell him, "No, I will eat just about anything you will cook for me. It is really very nice to have someone else cook and I am not picky at all."

He frowns at me but carries on with finding something to feed me. I keep sipping my tea and the pain in my head is beginning to recede. I am finally able to hold my head up without a hand on it. There is a slight lump just inside my hairline, but I think it will be fine. I watch him move through the kitchen. He is making an entire meal. I see he has a knife in hand and vegetables waiting to be cut on the counter, he must be looking for a cutting board. "There isn't one." He looks surprised. I continue on, "Charlie thought cutting boards were a waste of time with concrete countertops. So he forbid them in the house."

Devon's jaw drops, "Fate, I don't want to speak ill of your husband but this is very confusing to me. Why would you let someone tell you what to do in your own kitchen?" I stare deep into my nearly empty cup of tea as he goes back to meal prep.

"I don't know. Right now it seems like I was sleep-walking most of these forty years, it just never mattered to me that he was as domineering as I am now seeing that he was in all reality. This entire house is all Charlie. The colors, the placement of everything. I have changed almost nothing because it really didn't matter. I don't think I even saw it for the most part."

I look up at him, "Until you walked back into my life and woke me up. I wonder if I should be mad at you for waking me from the dream?" I feel a tear slip down my face.

Damn traitorous eyes. Then Devon's arms are around me as he murmurs "I'm so sorry" over and over again.

I find myself crying on his shoulder and I am a little frightened at these wild emotions that seem to be bubbling up since he walked into my library. The tears don't last long and I am embarrassed by them so I shoo him back to cooking before he burns my food. I stand very slowly and carefully, testing the waters to see if my head is ok for this.

No spinning or pounding, so I start to walk slowly toward the bathroom in the hall. I close the door behind me and lean carefully down to turn on the faucet and splash my face. The last thing I want right now is leftover evidence of my tears. I grab one of the towels that weren't supposed to be used to dry my face.

I feel a tender spot near the top of my right temple. Pulling the cloth away from my face I see a minor bruise running along the line of bone that separates forehead from temple. It is long but relatively thin. I guess that and the lump are what knocked old memories loose in my head.

.   .   .

THEY ARE ALL STILL FLOATING in there, but they seem to be starting to coalesce into a sort of order. I think they will over time and I just need to wait. I need to talk to my coven sisters. They could help. But not tonight. Tonight I will be fed, body and soul, by this gorgeous dark man creating a meal for me, find out if he picked up my glasses, and sleep.

Because today has been entirely too much. With my course decided I look at the towel in my hands, Charlie would demand it go in the hamper to be washed. I hang it back up where it was but sloppy. It makes me smile as I open the door and walk carefully back to the table.

8

He created an entire meal for me. Looking at it, I realize I haven't bothered to cook for myself in, well, since Charlie died. Yellow rice, honey and curry chicken, with a small salad and every dressing I had in the fridge set out. I glance at the kitchen expecting to see a mess but he has cleaned up after himself too. I don't know what to do with all this. I pick up a fork and knife, beginning to eat just to avoid my own feelings for a moment.

The food is fantastic. Mouth safely occupied with chewing, I look over toward him, only to see he is watching me eat and hasn't made himself anything. I quickly finish chewing, "The food is fantastic. Why aren't you eating? Aren't you hungry?" He cocks his head to one side and gives me a strange look, "Uh, no. I am not hungry right now, I ate earlier. So, not everything has clicked into place with your memories?"

I finish the bite I have just taken before answering, "No, not entirely. Right now it just feels a bit like I have a jumble of pictures floating in my head, but nothing holds still long enough for me to get a good look at it. Or when it does, it's like a random sound bite. The tongue thing, that is one of the random things that I got to be pretty immersed in. Other things," I shrug, "they slip away even as I try to hold on. Like water through my fingers. It's annoying and frustrating. I got a knock on the head and it gave me access to all these memories, sort of, if I don't really want to pay attention to them."

He nods, "I see. Hmm. Oh, looks like you've finished eating, let me get that for you." He whisks my completely empty plate away to the sink where he washes, dries, and puts it all away. I had no idea men did this kind of thing for any reason. This is wild. He has opened some wine and is filling a couple glasses. I hope it is sweet, I hate the fancy wines Charlie loved that taste like an oak tree. We aren't allowed to put trees in the taco meat, why is it in my wine?

He brings a glass over to me and seats himself in his chair once again. "Don't worry, it is a sweet wine. That is one of the few things that has never changed with you. There hasn't been one life in which you cared for a wine that wasn't sweet, so I figured it was a fair bet that you preferred them this time around as well." I exhale in relief, "Oh thank goodness. I didn't want to be rude, especially after you went to the trouble of making me a complete meal for me. No guy has ever done that for me—"

"Wait a minute, forgive me for interrupting but I can't have heard you correctly. Did you say no guy has ever made a meal for you?"

"Yes, that's what I said, why?"

He just shakes his head for a minute, "Because I find it amazing and horrifying that someone could have been married to you for so long and never once made a meal for you. This is the first time in this life that I have made you a meal, sure. But I have made you meals so many times in other lives, I don't understand how... Why wouldn't he do something so basic as make you a meal?" He holds up a hand, "You are not in any way obligated to answer that, I am expressing my amazement is all. I am happy to listen if you would like to tell me about it, but there may be more outbursts from me as I attempt to wrap my head around this."

I laugh, his face is so incredulous and I think he must feel the way I was feeling as he made me dinner. The laughter pours out of me until it is tears and I am crying on his shirt again.When finally my tears have dried I am exhausted.

The day, well night, has been so long. I check my phone, it is already near eleven. "I need to get some sleep. If you plan to sleep here, you are welcome to any room with a bed in it except mine. I am not ready for that, especially with all the stuff in my head right now."

I stand and begin to walk slowly to my bedroom

when he says, "I wasn't trying to find you this time. I wanted to leave you alone so that you could lead a regular life and live out your full measure of years. For all that, I am not sad I found you and now, I wonder if I didn't do you a disservice by not coming to find you." I nod, he may be right but I can't think on that tonight or the tears may come back.

Snotting his shirt up twice in one night is plenty. Once in my room I shut the door and strip down, throwing my clothes straight to the floor for tonight. I want nothing more than to rest and forget for a time all that has happened today.

MY DREAMS ARE CLOUDED, there is a man in the shadows. He caresses me but I do not want him; I turn away from him. Still he persists, he whispers in my ear and it sickens me. He bites me and I scream; he hisses and leaps away.

Devon runs into my room and jumps onto the bed, standing over me, facing away from me, "Where is it? What attacked you Fate? What happened?" I am frightened by the dreams I just had and by the boxer brief clad behind standing over my prone form, speech is beyond me. Seeing nothing but an open window and bedroom empty of all but me, he steps down off the bed and reaches over to turn on the lamp next to my bed.

Sitting down he asks me again, "Fate, what happened?" Blinking from the light I tell him, "I was dreaming. There was a man in the shadows of my dream. He was caressing my arms and my shoulders, I didn't like it so I turned away from him and he bit me." Devon's pupils expand and his nostrils flare, he glances at the open window before asking, "Where did the man in your dream bite you Fate?"

I am a little scared to tell him, he looks so angry, so I point toward the back of my neck on the right side. He says very gently, "May I see the spot please?" I can tell he is restraining his temper, and it is tickling something in my memories that just won't quite step into the light.

I roll toward the left a bit and Devon sweeps my hair ever so gently away from my neck; it feels like heaven. Then he hisses on an indrawn breath, I look back to see his face. His beautiful sepia skin is paler, more like an umber. His teeth are bared and brows drawn low, are his eye teeth longer?

"Fate honey, someone bit you." He tells me this in a voice that sounds smooth, like satin wrapped around the steel of a blade. "What do you mean someone bit me? Someone was really here? It wasn't a dream?" I hear my voice rising on each syllable, but I can't seem to stop it. He gathers me into his arms, "Don't worry little love, I am here and I will stay with you while you sleep. I will be a model of virtue, you have nothing to worry about on that account. For now, let's clean this blood off you, it's driving me crazy."

There's that tickle again, a memory just out of reach.

I am too tired to give a damn right now though. He

and I walk to my connected bathroom, I grab a washcloth and turn on the tap, waiting for warm water as I tell him, "If you look in the cabinet over there you will find some cotton balls and alcohol. Maybe even a band-aid or two." He obediently rummages through the cabinet to collect the items while I prep the washcloth with soap and warm water.

I lift my hair to clean the back of my neck and suddenly Devon is there behind me, I see him appear in the mirror and I yelp. He catches the cloth I dropped and says, "Allow me." He is so gentle. Dabbing and lightly wiping at my neck. He is very intent on the injury, I am fascinated watching him in the mirror. Once he finishes with the cloth, he grabs the closest towel and pats it dry. A brief sting from alcohol on the cotton ball and he is done. I am still watching as he tosses the cotton ball at the trash, licks his lips and kisses the spot.

It tingles briefly but I forget that as he says, "There you go, all better. Do you still want to sleep in here or would you prefer we move to another room?" I look toward my bedroom. The bed where Charlie and I slept for years. "You know, I don't think I could sleep in another room. This is the only place I have changed anything. The rest of the house is too red. I have the soft blues and purples on this bed. It is fine if you sleep here, I won't be upset over that. In fact," I look down because this isn't easy to say, "I, uh, I would be um, comforted, if we could cuddle?" I cut my eyes to the mirror to see his face and no luck. Instead, I feel his arms slip around me.

I lean into him, it feels so nice. He murmurs into my ear, "I would like nothing better." I sigh in relief, "Oh good. I thought you might not want to without the promise of anything else." He sighs, "I will never treat you like that Fate. I am so sorry I didn't come find you. I thought I was doing a good thing." He squeezes me once and then says, "Come on, get yourself in bed. I am going to close that window and the bedroom door, I will be just a moment." Getting into the bed I turn the lamp off, he turns off the bathroom light and I swear he must have flown to do those things. I see the curtains sway and the door is shut. All the light is blocked once again and he is sliding his body into the bed with me.

I slide myself over and curl up with my head on his shoulder. This is my spot. "I'm not hurting you laying on your shoulder am I?" I mumble as I drift off. I feel the rumble as he chuckles, "Not once in two hundred years." I feel like that is a weird thing to say, but I am too tired to put my finger on just what is wrong with it.

9

The memories are still a little all over the place, but they are settling. I can look at some of them for a time. I can only hope at this point that they will settle down at some point. For now, I am getting ready for work. Devon is taking me. I still want to stop by the cemetery to see Charlie. I kind of feel the need to tell him off again.

Probably cathartic and helping me to avoid therapy bills. I haven't told Devon about this yet. I don't know quite know how to tell him that I stop by my dead husband's grave every day to talk to him. I look at my face in the bathroom mirror, yeesh. I do not want Natasha asking the questions this face is going to beg her to ask, so makeup it is. My dry skin won't allow for less than actually using a liquid, moisturizing foundation. I start to look around for my glasses and catch sight of them in the mirror.

On my head.

Of course.

I put the minimum amount of makeup on that I can get away with after having the day I had. Which also means I have to cover up the bruise...ugh. Twenty minutes later and I have done all I am going to do. I step out of the bathroom, grab my purse and wander through the house looking for Devon. I smell coffee and head for the kitchen.

He turns as I walk in, "I made you coffee, since you have it and it smells fresher than six or seven months ago I figure you drink it at least occasionally. I also thought that the past day might call for it. Do you like cream or sugar?" I am floored, and in my head I see a memory of him from another time kneeling next to me as I lay in a bed. He was holding a cup of coffee and running his fingers lightly down my arm to wake me.

I blink the image away and say, "Yes. Um, both please. Two spoons of sugar and a lot of cream." I start to run a hand over my face, remember I have a face full of makeup and stop myself just in time. He has the coffee thing well in hand so I sit down at the table, glancing at my watch I see I have plenty of time. He brings the coffee over, setting it in front of me before he sits down in the chair next to mine. I sip my coffee to keep myself from blurting things nervously.

He pulls out his phone and begins doing some things on it, I am grateful for his lack of expectations. It gives me time to sip my coffee and focus my thoughts. Admittedly they are mostly about him right now, but he is not the entirety of what I need to focus on. In just the matter of a few hours around Devon, I feel like I need to re-evaluate my entire marriage. My life.

My coffee is not stirred quite enough so I move my finger in a stirring motion over it with just a brief pulse of magic. The brew spins, stirring all the sugary goodness up from the bottom. "I had wondered if you would be a witch in this life as well. I know you said yes last night in the library, but this is the first time I have seen you use any magic at all. Why don't you have your home warded against intruders?"

I look up in surprise, "Oh... well. Charlie didn't like magic. It creeped him out, he said. So I didn't do any around him. He thought I was part demon because I could do things. I just did my magic when I got together with my coven sisters." I look around this house that I am liking less and less, "I think I may need to sell this place. I don't live near them because he didn't like the neighborhood they lived in. If I am really honest, I think he didn't want me to have them so close. Probably felt that they would wake me up to his garbage if they saw it as often as they would have if we lived close. I think I would like to live near them, it would be nice to maybe walk across a yard to see them."

I set my cup down and turn to face Devon, "I have a ritual that I do every day. It is one that I am not ready to let go of yet so, um, yeah. I stop by the cemetery every day to talk to Charlie. Right now I really have a lot to say to him and I need to stop by there. Will you take me there today or should we leave now so I will have enough time to go there after I get to my own car?"

He cocks his head to the side, "Of course I will take you there. Honestly, I don't terribly like the idea of you being alone right now. Since you have been attacked twice in the past twelve or so hours." I nod, "Well, okay then. I expected that to be more awkward. What is wrong with you? You must have some kind of giant glaring fucking flaw somewhere, you can't possibly be this great and nothing at all that makes me crazy." Devon throws his head back and laughs long and loud. I pick up my coffee and finish the rest while he laughs.

Standing I say, "Ok, well, I see the thing now. Let's go laughing boy." I grab my purse and we walk out to his car, I put my hand on the door and remember I haven't locked the door again. I walk back over to the door and lock it while Devon watches with an enormous grin. I give him a look and he does his best to calm his grin but is less than successful.

THE CEMETERY IS quiet and empty. I am grateful. I direct Devon as he drives through. Once we are close, he stops and turns the car off. "Where would you prefer I wait?" I look over at him, "Here please. I wouldn't feel comfortable bringing you there just yet. I don't care if you hear me or anything, stand outside the car if you like. I need the space though."

"No problem, I will stand next to the car then. I'd like to be available should there be an issue."

I nod as I get out of the car and walk over to Charlie's grave. Stopping at the foot of his grave, I stare at his head-stone for a few minutes, reading the words over and over. Loving Husband.

"Why Charlie? Why did everything have to be your way? Why didn't I ever notice? How could I have been so blind? You know what? I am going to sell that house. It is huge, and we never needed that much space. You wanted it for appearances. I don't want to try living a fresh life in the house I spent so many years not living in, Charlie. Did you even like the person I am? You insisted I not do or display any of what makes me who I am. I changed the bedspread and sheets as soon as you were in the ground, Charlie. I despised that awful pattern of red and gold you insisted was perfect for our bed. I gave the set to the Goodwill. Along with all your clothes. I think tomorrow is the day I go through your office. I wonder what I will find in there?"

I stoop to pluck the dead flower off his tombstone, "Would it make you nervous? I know how much you wanted me to stay away from it and that has kept me out of there for nearly a year, but that is over."

I turn to leave but stop, "One other thing Charlie, I am going to do lots of magic in that house before I leave.

Fuck you for insisting I keep that part of myself hidden for so long and fuck me for going along with it."

Feeling lighter than I have in years, I walk away from the grave and back to Devon's car. "We can go now, I feel better." Devon nods and gets into the car as I do. The drive to work is quick in his Audi. He stops in front of the library doors to let me out. I look over at him as he stops the car, suddenly nervous.

He smiles at me, "Go to work Fate, I won't kiss you for the first time in this life as I drop you off at your place of employment. When I kiss you, it will make you weak in the knees and you won't be fit for work after. I need a change of clothes and to do a couple other things before I come back tonight. I will see you in a few hours."

I smile in relief, "That sounds nice. It will give me some time to talk with Natasha about the attack. I would hate for that to happen to her. See you later, Devon." I get out of the car, shut the door and trot up the stairs to the first set of doors. I turn and wave at him as I pull one of the doors open, stepping into the peace that is a library.

10

I have been at work for all of an hour when Charles comes strolling in. Unfortunately Natasha isn't here tonight, a fact I had completely forgotten until I was clocked in. I do have another librarian here, but she is about as magical as the book cart. Not very reassuring if I need backup. Though I have heard rumors that she is packing in that purse she keeps so close to her.

I continue on with my work at the desk, leaving Anelle to answer to whatever specious request Charles has tonight. Next thing I know Anelle is standing next to me telling me that the "nice man at the counter" wants to speak with me. I roll my eyes, groan, and thank her. Stepping over to the counter, I can feel him watching me. I refuse to look at him until I get to the counter itself. "What is it you need now, Charles? I have work to do."

He smiles indulgently at me, I want to stab him with an ice pick. "Why Fate, you wound me. All I need is you.

Did you have it appraised?" I tip my head to the side and scrunch my face, "Did I have what appraised?" He sighs, "The ring silly girl. Did you have it appraised?"

Oh Sweet Lady, I do not have the patience for this baboon tonight. "No Charles, I did not. Because I don't want the ring. I told you that last night. Are you quite sure you won't take it back? It seems a shame for it to be relegated to the back corner of a drawer because you gave it to the wrong woman." He shakes his head, "No sweet Fate, that ring is for you and you alone. I would love to see you wear it." He smiles at me again, "Come on, at least try it on. It won't hurt anything to try it on. Maybe you will like the way it feels on and it won't need to collect dust in a drawer."

Now I am the one sighing at this point. "Charles, I need you to go do whatever it is you do that doesn't involve me. I have work to do and I am absolutely not playing this game with you today." His bottom lips pops out in a ridiculous pout and he hangs his head briefly, "Well, fine. But I do care for you Fate, the least you could do is tell me what happened to your temple." My hand races to my temple, "Damn. I must have smudged the makeup off. It really isn't your business, but I bumped my head on the car. Now go away. I have things to do."

He eyes me like he knows what actually happened, "Here Fate, this is my card. If you run into anymore cars and need help, please call me. I won't be staying tonight, I have other obligations. Tomorrow I will be bringing you a gourmet lunch from my favorite place. You'll love it." He reaches across the counter to grab my hand and place his card in it when I make no move to take it from him.

I snarl at him, "You are infuriating. I don't want your lunch. I don't want your ring. I sincerely wish you would find a different library to haunt." I may as well have been talking to myself for all the good it did. He just waved as he walked out the doors. His arrogance knows no bounds and I don't know how I am going to get it through his thick skull that I am not interested. A shadowed memory of one of the times I was killed floats through my mind. Something in it seems so familiar, but it doesn't stick around to be analyzed. I look at the card in my hand, nothing but a phone number. How full of yourself do you have to be to force cards with nothing but your phone number on them into the hands of unwilling women?

THE NIGHT HAS BEEN WONDERFULLY quiet since Charles left. I have gotten a couple carts worth of books reshelved, Anelle has been scanning them in and putting them on one cart while I shelve the books from another. I am just on my way to swap carts with her when I feel Devon come into range of this weird connection we seem to have.

He is still driving and these books won't shelve themselves. Or... I look around the library, hmm, nope. There are still people here and nobody is going to be okay with books floating to their places on the various shelves.

The far end of the library is where he finds me. There was a deep pull to go toward him as he entered the library, but I resisted it. I guess he didn't because he is here in all that glorious flesh. Good night, he is hot! Those shoulders have me melting in all the special places. "Hello Devon. Get all your errands taken care of this evening?"

His brow scrunches a bit as he tips his head slightly, "Yes. I got everything taken care of that had to be done. I was thinking, now that we have slept together," my eyes narrow as he grins, "perhaps you will let me take you out to breakfast?" Looking down at the cart allows me to avoid his eyes while I think about this. I really would love to go to breakfast with him.

I also don't want to get involved with anyone, but I am already so involved with this guy. I have all these crazy memories floating in my head of the two of us from other times and these memories say that we belong together in a way Charlie and I never did. Devon is so different from Charlie too. He is so much kinder and caring. He is waiting with the utmost patience right now for me to answer him.

I look back up to find him watching me with sad eyes. How could I say no to those eyes? Sweet Lady help me, I can't. "Yes Devon, you can take me out to breakfast in," checking my watch I see it is already six, "two more hours when I get off work. I have to get this finished. Excuse me," I say as I push the cart around him. This is the last cart and I want to finish it before I leave. He chuckles at my retreating back, I want to go back and kiss him senseless while doing really dirty things with him in the stacks. Work, get the work finished.

I WALK OUT of the library into the bright morning. Thank goodness that most students are at their classes by the time I get out of the library. I look across the parking lot, to the space where my Devon-sense tells me he waits for me. He is sitting on the hood of his car. The sun adds a red hue to his sepia skin. Another memory flits through my mind. He is darker but more red and looks in pain?

Ugh. Why won't these memories sit still and behave? Annoyed now, I find myself stepping a little more forcefully than necessary and his brows raise in silent question. Smiling at him to let him know all is well, I pay more attention to not stomping about like a pouting child. As I get close he stands, "Where shall I take you for breakfast Fate?" Oh man, do I tell him where I really want to go? Will he hate it like Charlie did? Fuck it. "I would really love to go to the Waffle House."

I watch him closely in case he hates the idea and now me, but he smiles. He smiled about the Waffle House? "You're ok with that?" He tells me, "I would take you anywhere you wanted. If Waffle House is what you want, that is where we go. Shall we?" He sweeps his arm out toward the passenger side of his car. I walk past him to the door, he manages to reach around me and open it before I can touch it.

I seat myself in his comfy car, he closes the door and is quickly in the driver's seat. His driving is much faster than I remember from yesterday but my mind was pretty well gone for the entire trip so any judgements about his driving may be a lot skewed. He parks his Audi in the Waffle House parking lot and getting out he waits for me at the back of the car. We are lucky and find an open booth toward the front of the building.

Devon sits with his back to the wall, so I take the seat opposite. This place is pretty quiet for this time of morning, it makes me a little nervous about the food. But maybe we just caught them during their slow time. I place an order for coffee with a plate of steak, eggs over easy, and grits. I ask for rare, though they invariably do not get it right. I don't care though. Devon orders only coffee.

I wait till the waitress leaves to ask him why he doesn't get some food. He tips his head to one side and tells me, "I ate earlier before I came to the library. I had quite a few things to get done and I had a giant steak with baked potato while I was at it." I nod, "I see. You didn't have to take me out knowing you wouldn't be hungry. I kind of feel bad, we could have done this another morning." The waitress comes back with our coffees and a bowl of creamers. I thank her and turn to adjusting my coffee to just the way I love it.

Devon sips his black and says, "I am happy to finally

have you out with me, whether or not I eat is irrelevant. Now, back to our conversation from earlier. So you are a witch in this life too, correct?" I look around. After living so long with Charlie's insistence that I hide for fear of being ostracized or worse, I am not comfortable with just blurting things out. "Yes, I am. My entire family was, though the only one left now is my sister Prudence." I giggle, "She hates when I use her full name. Anyway, it runs in the family from what I understand. I inherited mom's family magic while my sister inherited dad's family magic. Why do you ask?"

The waitress has impeccable timing and chooses then to bring my food over and check to see if there is anything she can get for Devon. I think she might be a little hot for him, I can't blame her. I know he makes me hot sitting over there all dark and gorgeous. I cut up my entire steak, then my eggs. Once everything is bite-size pieces, I stir it all together. The first bite is glorious. It has been so long, oh how I have missed this place. I hear Devon snickering across from me, I give him a glare. "Find something funny mister?"

He laughs outright, "First, I find it adorable and humorous how much you are enjoying this meal. Second, you have egg on your face, just there." He points to the left of my mouth and I quickly grab a little napkin to clean it off. He continues, "I ask because I want to know about you Fate. You are a new person every time you come back in a lot of ways, even though your core personality stays the same. Every time you have been born since I met you, you have been a witch. The quick answer would be that I wanted to know if that was still true. The more truthful one is that I was hoping you were so that you would be better able to protect yourself. As a witch you can ward your home so that none may enter without your permission. I thought perhaps you weren't this time since your home is not warded. I know we touched on that earlier, but we didn't really talk about it and mostly I want to talk you into warding your house so you will be safe." I chew slower to give myself time to think.

He is absolutely right about the ward, and I don't know why I haven't set one. Swallowing the bite, I take a sip of my coffee and say, "You are absolutely right. I don't have a good reason for why it isn't warded now. Before Charlie died, he was the reason. I felt that I needed to respect his wishes. Now, well, t has been so long, I don't think it occurred to me to do it. Not to mention, I am a librarian. My life is usually much more quiet that it has been recently."

I finish my meal as we talk about random other things, I think he noticed it made me a little sad talking about why I hadn't handled my witchy business.

Leaving the restaurant, I smile to myself as the waitress tries to give Devon her number. He politely declines, leaving her sad. I tease him on the way out to the car and he laughs with me. Goddess, this is so nice. This is what I love about relationships, the normal stuff. How did I live for so long thinking Charlie was giving me this??

11

Devon drives me to my house with the promise that he will come get me tomorrow to pick up my car. At my house he walks me to the door, I unlock it and then leaving it standing partly open I turn to say goodbye. Devon takes me in his arms and presses his sweet lips to mine, I am enveloped in his scent.

My arms wrap around him of their own accord as I kiss him. What starts as warm kisses quickly turns into a raging storm of desire. My mouth opens to his and time stops while we kiss.

We come up for air dazed, my lips feel swollen and what a lovely feeling that is after so long. Devon regains control first and says, "Before I respect your wishes and go home to my very lonely bed, would you mind if I check your house to be sure no one waits inside?" Incapable of coherent speech, I nod and push the door further open. He steps in before me, stiffens and is suddenly a predator padding his way through my house. I follow closely behind, air called to me in case my visitor has returned.

Nothing appears to have been moved until we get closer to my bedroom. Then I can smell the flowers. The air is saturated with them. My bedroom door stands open and Devon steps inside so quietly I would swear he wasn't moving if I wasn't watching him. This is the guy to rob a house with if I were inclined toward that sort of thing. I watch from the doorway as he checks the entire room.

I stay focused on him because I am really sure I don't want to look at the flowers. This is so beyond creepy. How is this my life? Devon comes back out of my closet and heads for the bathroom, if anyone is still here that is the only place left they could be. Bad day for them if they are waiting in there. Devon comes back out moments later, "No one is here anymore."

I HAVE no choice but to look at the damn flowers now. I start with the floor. Some are crushed from Devon's feet but the pink roses there spell out 'I love you'. My eyes slowly drift up to my bed. There are red roses covering my pillows and the entire top half of the bed. The bottom half spells out 'Marry me Fate' and just then my breakfast is done with me. I run for the bathroom and make it to the toilet just in time. Everything I ate this morning boils up and into the bowl under my face.

Devon is there, pulling my hair back out of my face,

rubbing my back. Once the heaves stop I stand upright again, one hand pressed to my forehead and another on the countertop. Devon brings a cool, damp cloth and wipes my face. Feeling a bit more recovered, I turn to the sink and grab the mouthwash. Waffle House does not taste near so good the second time around, as many a drunken fool could testify.

Mouth rinsed and my stomach done rebelling, I ask Devon, "Would you please go open the back door and the garbage back there?" He nods and is gone down the hallway. I step into the bedroom and call the air to gather up every single flower in this room.

Shortly there is a whirling dervish of roses spinning in my bedroom. I guide it down the hall, following in its wake. Out the back door and I watch as they all land in the bin whose lid Devon is holding open. As the last of them drop in, he lets go of the lid. By the time I step in the door he is behind me and closes it after he enters. I hear the lock click into place and remember, I can ward this place. I can put a stop to this kind of nonsense. That is exactly what I am going to do. I head for the spare room with my secret stash of witch necessities. The time has come to put aside Charlie's wishes.

I HAVEN'T WORKED spell craft alone in a long time and I need all of my sacred objects to focus my mind. The air stuff is easy, I use it all the time. Crafting a functional ward that will keep the creepers out? That requires a lot more from me. Stepping into the spare room, I use air to lift the bed and move it to the other side of the room without knocking over the nightstands that guard either side of it. Keeping the bed hovering over there, I step into the space where it usually sits.

Facing the wall with my toes just touching it, I take three steps backward, making sure that the steps are heel to toe. After the third step, I turn to face the closet and put my right heel in front of the toes of my left foot. Success! I feel the button under my shoe and press it. Behind me a small cubby raises up from the floor. I had it put in years ago. Charlie was being particularly onerous about my family heirlooms. He wanted me to throw away anything related to the craft. I couldn't do it, but I could make him think I did while I spent a lot of his money on hiding it.

I contracted a woman to put this in, and she did the carpet for free. She was also a witch married to a man that was afraid of the craft. She got her start in the business creating these for herself. Once she had it installed, I hid all my items inside and spent a lot of time mourning my lost items. Charlie bought it and was quite magnanimous after that. I think he bought me a necklace or something, another thing I never wore, as a consolation.

With the cubby fully raised I open the door by pressing on it lightly, it opens without a sound. I can feel Devon watching all this, but I ignore him for the time being. I won't be putting these back in here. I will be calling a realtor today, and Benjamin. Perhaps he knows a good realtor? I pull out the wooden box with the star carved on the top.

My mother said it was made from a rowan tree that grew on our great, great grandmother's land. It was felled by lightening one year and they salvaged what they could to create as many things as possible from it. My sister got the other box, the twin to this one. It is said that those who shouldn't touch it will receive a nasty shock for their troubles, but I haven't tested the tale.

I shut the door and gently push the top of the cubby down. It silently retreats into the floor as I stand. Walking toward the door, I send the bed floating back into place. As I get to the door Devon moves aside, he follows me as I walk down the hall to the kitchen. Try as he might, Charlie could never make the living room the heart of the house, it was always the kitchen.

I set my box down on the counter and placing a hand on either side of the lid; I open the box and rest the lid against the front of the cabinet. Incense, scrying bowl, locks of hair from myself and the women before me. A white-handled knife and a small wand, also from the rowan tree, tarot cards, and some inks made by my mother and some few other things. I remove the dragon's blood ink, incense, wand, and the knife. Devon is standing near when I turn away from the counter with items in hand. "I need you to back up a bit please." He takes himself off to the table and sits down to watch. I don't mind.

I call my book to me and some paper as well. Once the items reach me I keep them hovering while I sit on the floor of the kitchen. Setting down the objects already in my hands, I hold my hands out and let my book drift down into them and the paper onto the floor next to my knee. I call a quill to me, remembering that I need something to write with for the ward I want to cast. It lands in my hand point first, stabbing me because I wasn't paying attention. I drop it and ignore the snickers from the jerkface at the table.

It's been a while since I did this, I'm rusty. Leaving the traitorous quill where it lies, I open my book and search for my spell. Finding it, I set the book on the floor in front of me, with a small bit of air over it to hold it open. I study the spell a moment before I open the incense, flipping the lid over as I use it to hold a small amount of the powder. I call the lighter to me since I forgot that as well, but I pay attention as it sails in to me and catch it in my hand with no injury. I light the incense and set it off to the side with the lighter.

Quickly, I perform the rest of the actions required to set the ward around the house itself, with a small cushion between. As I finish the casting, I feel the ward snap into place and I remember how nice it was to do magic. I am a little sad for all the time I let slip away while I did no magic at all. My life was so gray already, I don't know how I let the only color in my life go so easily.

WITH MY WARD in place and my box put away in my bedroom, I stand and walk over to the table to sit with Devon. "Did you know that you light up when you do magic? It is the most beautiful thing I have ever seen." I blush, "No, uh, I was not aware of that. What I am aware of is that I have two phone calls to make and then I need to sleep." I look away, off toward the kitchen to ask, "Would you like to stay here with me today?" I look down, not willing to check to see if the idea horrifies him.

He reaches over and touches my chin with a finger, applying a gentle pressure to bring my face toward him. I allow it and finally drag my eyes up to look at his face, "I would love to stay here with you Fate. I would stay with you always. Wherever you go that is where I need to be more than anything. You are my fate, my love, and the one I would seek in the far corners of the planet for as long as I am on this planet. Never doubt that I live for your smile, my darling Fate."

A rogue bit of water steals its way down my face, "You can't go around saying things like that, you make my face leak." I say as I swipe away the moisture with the back of my hand. I call my phone to me, "I need to call my lawyer, and then a realtor. Hold those thoughts, and we will talk about what you can seek out as soon as I finish these calls." His face lights up with a smirk that makes me feel incredibly sexy.

Phone calls. Focus Fate. I tap the screen a bit and get the call started. Benjamin is fantastic. He says my in-laws have been by there multiple times this month trying different tacks to claim the house from me.

I tell him they can buy it from me if they want it that bad and he laughs, "Fate, I don't know if they could. Everything they have come up with is from the internet, they haven't brought a lawyer by at all. That may be because no lawyer will touch the case, but who knows. So you're going to sell the house?"

I nod, even though he can't see me, "Yes. I want to make a clean start. Have a little place of my own that my in-laws have never been inside of, ha. Mostly, this place is just too big for me." I reach over and take Devon's hand in mine while I talk with Benjamin.

He gives me the name of a good realtor and assures me that he will be happy to act as my attorney for the sale. We say our goodbyes and I call the realtor, Maggie. We set up a time for her to come by later today and then end the call as I need to get to sleep very soon.

I HAVE JUST one more thing I want to take care of before I go to sleep. Turning to Devon I say, "Would you like to go mess up my sheets?" He grins, "I thought you'd never ask."

12

I have not felt this content in years. I have places on my body that have never been so satisfied in my entire life. I stretch and sit myself up, Devon is sprawled across the bed with his arm hooked around my waist. My stretching pulls me away a bit, and he reflexively pulls me closer to him.

I remember that he usually wakes up hungry and hates cold blood. He always said it made him feel like he was drinking from a lizard. I'll be sweet this morning and put a bag in hot water to get it to temperature before he wakes up.

Sliding out of bed, the tasks I have just planned for myself hit me. Blood. Why would he need blood unless? NO! It can't be, he isn't; but the memories that have been so elusive are slamming into place one after the other. Devon drinking from a deer in the woods. Devon drinking from a man that attacked me in a past life. Devon drinking from a bottle we kept in the cellar. Myself putting one of those bottles to warm in a pot of water.

I think I might be sick, "Oh Goddess, what have I gotten myself into?" I make it to my closet and start yanking on clothing. What am I going to do? How can I have a relationship with someone that kills people on a regular basis? I have to get out of here before he wakes up.

I make it to the bedroom door but Devon is in front of me before I can open it, "Fate, what happened? What's wrong Fate?" He puts his hands on either side of my face and turns it so he can see my eyes, "Fate. What. Is. Happening. Talk to me. Whatever it is, we can do something about it together." I realized when he put his hands on my face that I have tears running down it, and I am terrified. But he is so gentle, so concerned...

"I see. Fate, you've just remembered what I am, haven't you?" I don't think I can speak just yet, so I nod. His hands move from my face to my shoulders, "Fate, love, you will never have to worry that I would bite you, in that manner. As for any other concerns, we have become much more cultured over the last few decades. Now we order out. The blood is all donated or from a farm. Donated human blood is ridiculously expensive, so most don't bother with it. The vast majority of vampires drink the blood of cows or pigs and some even will go for sheep's blood. It is rare for one of our kind to hunt people anymore and with the exception of the guy that tried to mug you, I haven't taken from a human since before you were born into this life."

His speech has given me time to calm down and knowing that he doesn't, wait — "You said there was an exception?" He looks down and away, "My temper got away from me when he attacked you,"

Devon walks over to his pants and begins putting them on, "and so I did drink from him till he died. I put the body in my trunk for safekeeping until I could dispose of him properly. If it makes you feel better, he was a vampire. So I wasn't drinking from a regular person or anything."

He zips his pants up and I am a little sad, he is a snack. "So you ate the guy that attacked me?" His eyes open wide and his jaw drops a little, "No. I ate you earlier today. I drank from him. There is a sizable difference." He crosses his arms over his chest and stands there daring me to say differently and I have this crazy urge to taunt the vampire.

"Isn't that like saying tom-A-to or tom-AH-to? The difference is so slim as to not be a difference?" I want to laugh, but that is really going to spoil my game.

He looks so floored by what I said, "I think maybe you just aren't secure enough to call a duck a duck here." I open the bedroom door and start down the hall, managing not to snicker until I clear the door.

Then he grabs me in a bear hug from behind, "You're teasing me aren't you? Little minx!" He tickles me in the one spot I am ticklish, just above my hip bone. No one else has ever found that spot! Very shortly I am reduced to a giggling puddle in his arms and begging for mercy. He stops tickling me and picks me up.

Goddess love a brawny man! He pulls me close to him, "I love you Fate Owens, even with your awful sense of humor."

I laugh and kiss his cheek, "Let me down, mister. I need coffee and a bathroom, though not in that order." He laughs but releases me, "I'll get your coffee love, you go to the bathroom. The house isn't going to sell if you start peeing on the carpets." I laugh at him as a head back to the bedroom and my bathroom.

A few minutes later I enter the kitchen, and he hands me a cup. I take a sip and it is glorious. He can stay just for his coffee making ways. "Oh Devon, if I wasn't already hooked on you this coffee business would certainly do it. You, sir, are a fabulous coffee maker."

He chuckles at my glowing assessment of his coffee prowess before his face goes serious, "Are you really ok with everything now or in shock?" I sigh and go sit myself at the table. He follows and sits across from me.

"I am as okay as I can be right now. Yes, I am really messed up with this idea. I didn't even realize that vampires existed. All the memories that slammed into place this morning tell me otherwise, but they also, now that I am calmer, tell me that you are not going to hurt me or anyone either of us cares about. For that matter, the memories tell me that you are the most stand-up guy I have met in any lifetime. And I remember everything. Including how I died."

He pales at that but I continue anyway, "I don't recall the face of the guy that killed me. I do recall that I lived other lifetimes before the one I met you in. They aren't as bright though, more like this one before you showed up in my library." My coffee begs to be enjoyed and I am not going to tell it no.

As I sip my coffee he speaks, "What do you mean they aren't as bright? That this one wasn't as bright?" One more sip of my coffee to tide me over till I can return my attention to it, "I mean they all seem a little gray. How does life feel to you when I die? Or have been dead for a while and you haven't found me yet? For me, it feels like part of me isn't here. Like I am going through the motions but not really there." He nods and I turn back to my coffee.

It is at a point where I need to devote my attention to finishing it before it goes cold. Nobody likes cold coffee that was meant to be hot. Or no one I know does. Devon must have known I just wanted to finish my coffee as he remained silent till I drained the last drop. "I think I do understand what you mean. When you die, it is a bit like some of the color drains out of the world and nothing is as important as when you are part of my world. Even my projects are less important when you aren't here." He looks off to stare out a window at the back yard.

I tell him, "I think you do understand. It is more

pronounced in the memories though. With those it is a lot like having full color movies alongside black and white films. It's a little disconcerting, but I will make it through. Now, I do have some bad news for our fresh sex life." He turns a stricken face to me, I hold up my hands, "Don't worry, it isn't anything terrible." He exhales in relief and I giggle, "Tonight is the night that everyone comes here for girl's night. Pru, Memré, Natasha; they are all going to be here and you can't be here. In part because we are going to discuss you in great detail. Also because part of that conversation is that we are going to discuss the sex we had last night in significant detail as well."

He grins, "Well, I feel like a made a good impression in that respect at least."

I smile, "Yes, you did that. But I am not the only one that thinks vampires aren't real. And the reactions may not be great at first. Which is why it will be better if you are not here. Oh NO!" I clap my hand over my mouth as Devon jumps up and looks around for a threat, removing my hand I tell him, "Shit, I just remembered that my sister Pru can read my mind. Something like watching a movie. She is going to see us having sex, and that a guy that broke in here too. Oh man," I cradle my head in my hands as Devon laughs, "they are definitely bringing booze over tonight. There is no way I am getting through all these explanations without booze."

Devon is still laughing, I think briefly about smacking him but it wouldn't do any good and would likely break my hand.

He manages to rein in the laughter to ask, "How would you feel if I showed up tomorrow afternoon with coffee, croissants and aspirin?" I look up at him, "I would feel like you deserve the opportunity to mess up my sheets again, good sir. Though it would have to be after the coffee and croissant."

He smiles at me and the afternoon just lights up. How does this guy have such an effect on me? I know the witches agreed to bond us but I begin to think their agreement was only because they saw it happening with or without their aid. I lean out to watch him walk down the hallway, he has got such a nice ass. I bet I could bounce a quarter off of it.

He disappears into my bedroom, and I sit back in my chair. After he leaves I am getting a shower and cleaning this place up a bit. Oh, and the realtor should be here in... I check my watch, another two-and-a-half hours. Perfect. The house will look great by then and so will I.

Devon saunters back out of the bedroom with his shirt on and shoes in hand, I laugh. "Ah, the afternoon walk of shame. Love it." He laughs, "I would do naked shame walks daily if it meant I got to be with you Fate." Oh goodness, that's a picture. I get up and walk over to hug him. Dropping his shoes he wraps those big arms around me and squeezes me close with his hands, each on a cheek. He lifts me a bit and I wrap my legs around his waist as we kiss. My hands roam his massive shoulders, my nails beginning to lightly dig in as he pulls me tighter to his body, I can feel his erection as it grows.

We come up for air as I rock my pelvis against his and he groans, "Oh god Fate, I can't leave if you do this." I grin, "Just wanted to make sure you had an excellent reason to come back." His lips meet mine in a rush and he murmurs against my lips, "I will always come back for you Fate." He walks us over to the couch as we kiss like it has been a century or so since we saw each other last.

He kneels in front of the couch with my legs still wrapped around him and moving his hands to my waist he pushes gently till I unhook my legs from around his torso and he sets me on the couch without ever breaking the kiss. I feel his hands at the waistband of my pants just before he snatches them down under my butt and off my legs.

I hear his zipper and then I feel him pressing into my core. I am so wet for him that he glides in with ease as my hungry body expands to allow for his size. Fully inside me, he holds still for just the barest moment while he moves his hands back to my butt cheeks, cupping them firmly. He pulls back slowly and then starts pounding into me with a ferocity I love.

I moan in ecstasy as his thrusts hit just the right spot. My moans spur him to greater heights and I am falling off the cliff of delight, the world exploding in a rainbow of colors as he joins me. The pulsing of our bodies the only movement we can stand for long moments and even that is almost too much.

Long minutes later we drift slowly apart as he says,

"There is no force on earth that could keep me from coming back to you."

DEVON FINALLY MAKES it out the door with the promise to have someone drop my car off here for me. I watch him leave as I text the girls, *Bring booze*.

13

emré is first to arrive. She brings pineapple rum and orange juice. Just as we get the glasses out, one of the others knocks on the door. Memré lets her in while I get out another glass. Prudence arrives before Natasha gets through the door and they wait for her to come in as well. Prudence doesn't even put her purse down before she heads to the kitchen with one question on her lips, "Who are these men that have been here?"

I set down the rum with a sigh. "Can we all have our drinks before we play five thousand questions? Hello sister, it would be great if you could at least kiss me before you mind-fuck me."

I don't even look over at her as I wait for the answer and I guess that said something to her because she dropped her purse on the table and set the rum and cranberry ginger ale she brought next to it then walked off.

Likely to use her psychic sense to snoop through my house. I have always had issues with her prying into my life with her psychic ability. In this case though, it could work out really well.

Maybe she can tell me if the guy that snuck in the house and bit me is also Charles the creepy from the library. Not that she would actually know who Charles the creepy is if she saw him, or well, I guess she would after creeping through my mind.

Of course she is also going to know about all the sex I had this morning and this afternoon, so that cat is out of the bag. I get drinks made for all of us, Natasha and Memré take theirs to the table. I bring mine and Pru's. We wait in silence for her to come back down the hallway and sit down with us.

As Pru sits down at the table, I push her drink over to her and she says, "Oh Fate, you have got some explaining to do. Why haven't you told any of us about this?" Natasha pipes in, "Well, if the guys are who I think they are, I kind of do know about them. She met them at work." Pru looks at me wide-eyed, "What are you doing at work these days, Fate?"

I shake my head, "Well, mostly I am stacking books but occasionally I find a guy and lure him home so I can rob him of his everlasting soul to feed my youth." Memré busts out laughing and her laughter is infectious. We all join her. Eventually I calm down enough to tell everyone what has been going on.

The creepy life that is Charles stalking me, the sneakin-the-window-biter that could be Charles, the magnificence that is sex with Devon and that is where the conversation went sideways oddly enough. "Wait. Wait. Wait." Pru throws her hands up in the stopping motion, "I need you to go slower here. I want a lot of details about this Devon guy because last we all," she circles her hand to include Memré and Natasha, "heard from you is that you are not doing the relationship thing ever again because you didn't want to go through the pain of losing someone like you did with Charlie. Now you're having mind blowing sex with a guy that you suddenly sound very serious about. And if what I saw is any sign, you are serious about him. The fuck Fate?"

Sigh. "I know. And I still feel that way. But Devon has a couple of things going for him that most guys wouldn't. The first one being that we were bound together in another life, neither of us is complete without the other one. We spend our lives searching or treading water if we aren't together. Considering what you all thought about my marriage to Charlie," they all look away over that, "I know which one you would say I was doing. And, well... you wouldn't be wrong."

Now it's my turn to look away. Take a deep breath and dive in Fate. "The other thing Devon has going for him is that he is, um, he's a vampire." I watch everyone for their reactions. Pru's face drains of color and the whitest girl here has now managed to out-white the white cabinets in the kitchen. Natasha just looks... guilty?

Ooo, what does she know? I meet her eyes and raise

my brows at her. She mouths "later" at me and I nod. Memré just looks very curious, I think she would rather I go back to the mind blowing sex stories. Makes sense, if I recall her husband was not the greatest in that respect and she hasn't dated since then. I think stories are as close as she has gotten since him. I would be content with that, but I think Pru needs to process the vamp thing.

While we wait I grab all our glasses and get us a refill. Pru is so quiet and pale, booze can only help that. Or not. Either way, I want another drink because I am still dealing with my life too. Drinks refreshed, I realize I do not have enough hands or sobriety to carry four glasses back to the table. I am still staring at the glasses when Memré comes over, "Are they doing tricks for you?"

She looks a little concerned for my mental health and well, I can't blame her. "I can't carry four glasses back to the table." She laughs at me, "Hon, have you eaten today? I'll carry a couple and that will solve your problem." She grabs her drink and another, leaving me with just the right amount to carry.

I grab them and start toward the table, "You know, I am not sure I did eat today. I had sex with Devon on the couch before he left, cleaned, met with the realtor... Nope. Food was not in the equation. Maybe I should order pizza. Would anyone like pizza?" Memré and Natasha say they would while Pru sits there still silent. She is drinking though and not so pale, I think she will be all right.

I head to the bedroom to order pizza while digging

through my purse for my wallet and glasses. I can't see the numbers without them, luckily the person on the other end only has to wait a little bit before I get myself together. They tell me it will be forty minutes or so and thanking them I hang up the phone to the sound of shouting in the kitchen.

I hear Pru saying it isn't right as I head back out and my heart sinks; she is the last person I thought would have an issue with this vampire thing. I walk in like I haven't heard a thing, Memré and Natasha look up as I enter and Pru cuts off a diatribe about dirty bloodsuckers.

"Well, I was hoping to pretend I didn't hear that Pru." She glares at me as I take my seat, "Then you shouldn't have mated with a vampire! Seriously Fate, what are you thinking? There is a reason why they hide from everyone. They are dangerous, disgusting bloodsuckers and they all deserve to die. Who knows what diseases they carry! This is why—" She cuts off whatever she was going to say but I don't care what it was to be honest.

I shake my head, "I cannot believe that a witch would say something so horribly bigoted Pru. Every woman in this room has spent her life hiding what she is because humans can't handle people with power they can't access or control. We witches have been hunted, burned, derided, and outcast for being what we were born to be. I am disappointed in you in a way I never thought I would be with one of my people."

Pru's jaw has dropped and by the end of my brief speech her face is leaking. She stands and excuses herself to the bathroom, leaving Memré and Natasha to give me sympathetic looks as I take a large swig from my glass.

The bell rings, and Natasha says she will get the pizza. I tell her not to step out the door; the ward doesn't extend past it. She nods and doesn't even question it; I love her. Pru and Natasha return at the same time. We forgo conversation for a bit in favor of scarfing pizza. Bellies sated, Memré volunteers to refresh the drinks this time.

Pru, picking at the pizza box, says, "fnkunvonoqgogqgindjkn." I look at Natasha to see if she has any clue what Pru just said, but she shrugs. "I'm sorry, what was that?" Pru looks up at the ceiling and we look up with her, nothing there. She sighs, grits her teeth, "I said I'm sorry. I didn't mean that and you're right. OK?" I look at her in surprise and she narrows her eyes at me, "You do not want to tease me about this Fate." I smile and shrug, "I don't suppose you have noticed it but I am processing things rather slow tonight."

Memré shouts from the counter, "She really is VERY slow tonight." My lips twist to the side, "Gee, thanks. I think... Anyway, making fun of you didn't even cross my mind. I accept your apology. And I guess I should tell you that he will be here in the afternoon with coffee, croissants, and aspirin because he is a real life prince like that. Also, I want him to meet you all."

Pru tips her head, "I didn't know they could be out in the sunlight?" I sip at my fresh drink courtesy of Memré-who-*can*-carry-four-glasses before I answer, "They can actually. I only know this because the unlocked memories have finally settled into place, but they have provided me with a lot of information. Vampire's eyes are more sensitive to the sunlight, so a bright day is fucking awful for them. They don't really die very often because they are just really difficult to kill. That is the biggest reason why I am okay with this relationship. I am more likely to die than he is, and that makes me feel a little safer." Thank Goddess they did not catch that slip.

But maybe I should tell them? Curse you booze for making decisions hard. "Um, speaking of that. There is a thing that you all should know. Someone has killed me in every life that I have found Devon in, usually not real long after we get together."

Three sets of very round eyes stare at me until Natasha says, "You might have mentioned that a little sooner." I shrug, "Honestly, I am more ok with a murderer after me than if they were after him or one of you." Natasha shakes her head at me while Memré manages to roll her eyes and take a drink.

She is so talented.

Pru glares at me. "Oh drink up Pru, I'm not dead yet. I certainly don't plan to make it easy on the dickface. This time I know and it will be different."

There are those big eyes again. "I remember things from all my past lives ever since someone tried to mug me and Devon ate them. He doesn't like it when I say it that way," I giggle picturing his face, "but, eat or drink the guy still ended up dead." Pru says, "Maybe I could get to like this guy." Cutting my eyes at her I continue on, "This time

I know that he is going to be looking to kill me. I can prepare and maybe," I look at my best people and take a deep breath, "maybe with some help I could off him this time? If I had help from you guys, I think we could keep me alive. I mean, Devon obviously hasn't done a bang-up job so far with this guy."

They are all looking at me like I have lost my mind, guess that's a no on the helping me stay alive. Damn. I was counting on them.

"How could you even think you have to ask?" Memré shakes her head at me, "Give me your glass. The women in this room are family, and family takes care of family. If one of us is threatened then we take care of that too." Heading to the booze counter she throws back, "I ought to cut you off the liquor. Can't believe you had to ask that question." Memré keeps on muttering about my lack of sense while I try not to cry.

My heart must have swelled up three sizes with love for these women that would have my back even through this. I couldn't have asked for a better family. We pass the rest of the evening talking about anything except the guy that wants to kill me.

Devon's prowess is discussed thoroughly, as is the issue that is Charles the creepy. Natasha assures me that she is going to file a report with the school, though we don't think it will do much good. Charles has made substantial donations to the university and most universities aren't willing to take a female employee's side over that of a wealthy donor harassing said employees. Whatever. Maybe we will just cast a spell to make his balls shrivel up.

Lowering those testosterone levels should have an effect. As morning draws near we all stumble down the hall to sleep in my giant bed. We never did this when Charlie was living but after he died, I was so lonely and heartbroken that they all spent a lot of time sleeping here with me and they just found it easier to be in the same bed with me when I had nightmares.

When girls nights came around we had all been sleeping in there at one point or another so we just went with it and that became the tradition, whatever house we are in for girls night everyone piles into one bed when it comes time to pass out. Honestly, I don't know how I would have made it through those first months without them. I think tomorrow is the day for Charlie's office to be cleaned out. It is time and past.

I feel I can let go of that room now, I don't have to leave it be to pretend he is in there anymore. Besides, I will have all my people with me tomorrow and that is truly what makes it just the right day to tackle that room. Besides, Charlie has a lot of stuff in that room. I had no idea one man could amass that much stuff in a home office but I do now. When I opened that door, oh the shock. For now, I need to get some sleep before afternoon arrives with Devon and coffee.

14

I wake to my brain working hard at pounding its way out of my skull. Where did it find a battering ram in there? Pushing the covers off I drag myself into an upright position. The pounding stops and I breathe a sigh of relief.

Standing is okay, a little wobble but nothing major. Then the pounding starts again. Wait, that pounding isn't in my head. It's coming from the front of the house? OH. Devon must be out there. Stumbling toward the front of the house I only hit the walls a couple times. Really not bad. Little peek out the hole before I open the door, I am in no condition to deal with the crazies today.

Definitely Devon out there.

Push off the door and turn the lock, you can do it Fate. I manage opening the door and there is my gorgeous vampire, standing there looking tasty with my coffee in his hand. Seeing the state I am in he plucks a coffee cup out of the tray in his hand, holding it out to me like an entrance fee. One sweet sip later and I can step back to allow him entry. In fact, I am going to allow him to kick the door shut too while I make my way to a chair at the table.

The glasses from last night still sit in mute testament to the cause of my current state of being. I look toward the counter and see that the rum still sits on the counter as does the last container of orange juice. Devon sets the tray of coffee down in a clear spot on the table, and shoving some glasses aside makes room for the brown bag he has in his hand. I watch through blurred vision and sip my coffee as he grabs all the glasses and heads toward the sink.

"Do you happen to see any glasses laying about?" Devon turns toward me, "What?"

More coffee in me for clarity, "I said, do you see a pair of glasses anywhere? I am not sure where exactly any of them are but there is probably a pair out here some-where. I don't have the coordination to find them right now." He laughs and does a slow circle before heading toward the far end of the kitchen.

Very shortly he has reached me and even more care-fully slides my glasses on to my face. I am not even mad that he didn't trust me to put them on. I probably would have lost an eye if I had done it. He opens the bag and the most wonderful smell in the world pours out, caressing my senses and waking my stomach.

I moan.

Devon reaches in the bag and pulls out what must be an award winning croissant. He hands it over to me and I take it like the priceless jewel it is. Just as I shove a large chunk of croissant in my mouth Natasha comes down the hall. Devon grabs a coffee and holds it out in her direction.

She takes the coffee, sits down next to me and says, "Well no wonder you're keeping him. He's a frickin' angel of mercy here. Hey, angel. Got any cream or sugar to go with this? I am not particular about where it comes from." Chuckling Devon reaches into the brown bag of heaven and pulls out a handful of creams and sugars. He hands those over to Natasha and reaches back into the bag bringing out another croissant that he holds out to her as well.

She doesn't notice it for a moment, being focused on her coffee. When she does look up she gives a little squeal of delight and takes the buttery goodness from him. Around a mouthful of the croissant she says, "I don't give a damn what anyone thinks about him, keep him. A man that brings coffee and croissants is worth his weight in gold."

I laugh, "No worries, I will be keeping him." Then my dear sweet Devon brings out the coup de gras from the bag, a fresh bottle of aspirin. He quickly opens the bottle and doles out a couple pills to each of us. Memré is next to wander out and he has her coffee on the table in front of a a chair alongside a croissant, cream, sugar, and two aspirin. "This is your sex guy from the library?" she asks as she seats herself in front of the layout. I nod, "Mmmhhmm." as I finish the last of my croissant.

She sips her coffee and says, "Any more of these just laying around up there?" Natasha and I break out in laughter as Devon comes to sit next to me after laying out one more setup for Pru.

I can only hope her initial attitude towards vampires from last night will not return, she is notoriously stubborn and slow to change her mind. If she doesn't accept the coffee and croissant I am taking hers. Those things were delicious.

Remembering my manners I introduce everyone, now that we are all some semblance of witch again. My friends are awesome, thanking him for the coffee and croissant. The table is mostly silent as we sip our coffees. I wonder if I am not the only one concerned about what Pru's reaction to meeting Devon will be.

Eventually I hear her moving around and I take a deep breath. This could be fine or it could be a shit storm. Pru stumbles out and seeing the empty chair with coffee and croissant she stumbles over and seats herself. A sip of coffee later she says, "Thanks Devon. This is divine." I let go the breath I didn't realize I had been holding. Devon reaches over and rubs my arm, I guess he knew I was holding my breath.

Pru glares at me, "I am not a monster Fate. I do have manners. And you did very quietly tell me what a jerk I was last night. I may be stubborn but that would be utter nonsense." Devon raises his brows and looks at me. I shrug, "I know you aren't a monster Pru. I still wasn't certain what your reaction would be to meeting him after how you said you felt about vampires last night."

She waves her hand at me as though she wanted to wave the whole comment away, "I worry for you. I don't want you to be vamp food. What if he decides to eat you too?" I giggle, "Well, considering how nice it felt last time I am probably going to let him."

Narrowing her eyes Pru says, "Not at all what I meant." I can hear Devon trying not to laugh as I say, "Yes, I know what you meant. The fact is that he is absolutely not going to bite me unless I ask him to do so. He is not someone you have to worry about. Our souls are bound, hurting me would hurt him too. I mean, look at this."

I gesture at the remains of all that Devon brought, "Do you ever remember Charlie doing anything like this? I don't. That was part of why you all hated him. He was incredibly selfish and his idea of being nice to me was to eat elsewhere without me if I was tired and didn't want to cook for him." I see Devon's jaw drop upon hearing that and he leans forward, "What do you mean he ate elsewhere without you?"

Sigh, here we go. Memré jumps in, "She means the jerk would literally leave her here and go out to have dinner alone if she was too tired to cook for him. He was a first class jerk in that way and a lot of other ways that had all of us wanting to curse him at various points during their marriage." Devon looks around for confirmation and even Pru is nodding in agreement. Shaking his head he turns to me, "I am so sorry I did not come find you sooner. I will never keep myself away from you again no matter how I think it might be good for you." He scoops me up and deposits me into his lap, hugging me close.

I lean into the firm wall of his chest and lay my head against his. "You're sweet, but it isn't your fault I settled." He tips his head back to look at me, "If I had sought you out when I felt you come back you would never have settled for a guy like that. You deserve so much better than that Fate, I am struck knowing that you were treated so poorly."

A chorus of "Aaaaawwws" emerge from my family, I look over at them as my cheeks light up with a blush. "Stop. You're making me blush. Fire engine red isn't a good look on me." They start laughing at me and standing up from the table they say that they need to get themselves home to get ready for work the next day. I leave Devon sitting there with one more touch of foreheads.

Entering my bedroom I see all of them sitting on my bed waiting for me with matching grins. I close the door behind me with a laugh, "Out with it ladies, what do we need to discuss?" They laugh at me and Natasha says, "Really, does he have any friends? I have been with vampires before and the stamina along with their attention to detail makes them the best lovers." Memré and Pru fall over laughing as I shake my head, "I don't know but I will definitely check in with him about that. Honestly, I haven't asked yet. We have barely spent two days together and those days have been pretty damned eventful. As I happen to know that none of you actually need to get home right now, I could use your help."

They all stop laughing and look to me, waiting patiently. I run a hand across the back of my neck, "I feel like it's time I go through Charlie's office. I am putting this house up for sale so I can buy something closer to—" I am cut off with the screams of joy and hugs from the three of them.

Once they have calmed down and I can be heard again; I continue on, "Like I was saying, I want to live closer to you all. I have to clean out his office at some point and since you all are here I was hoping you would do it with me. His office is the only space of his I haven't cleaned out since he passed." Pru throws an arm around me, "You know we will. We all have the rest of the afternoon and well into the evening free but it shouldn't take that long. Let's all get cleaned up and we can get to it."

I nod, "Thank you, all of you. I don't know what I would have done without you. I'm going to go let Devon know. You all go ahead and start with the showers. Natasha darts into the bathroom yelling out "DIBS!" as she goes. I laugh and retreat back out to the kitchen, let them fight it out. I have an on demand water heater, so endless hot water no matter how many showers happen.

Devon is still sitting at the table when I get to the kitchen. I walk over and sit straddling him, he groans.

Grabbing my hips he pulls me closer and sends a delicious shiver of desire through my body. I lean forward and give him a kiss that he quickly deepens. We come up for air and I remember why I came out here. "Oh my. You are a distraction." He grins at me and I work to get back on track.

"Anyway, with all my family here I decided last night that it is time to go through Charlie's office and get it cleaned out. It is the last holdout of his things and has to be cleaned out before I sell anyway. It is likely to be pretty emotional for me. If you don't feel like you can deal with that, I understand."

"I am not going anywhere Fate."

STEELING myself I open the door to Charlie's office and push it so the door swings open and I can take a minute before I step in. It looks like he stepped away just minutes ago. His computer sits there sleeping and his desk is neat as a pin.

A stack of papers in a metal wire basket on the left corner, his mail in another on the right. There are two filing cabinets standing tall behind his desk, like sentinels guarding all the things he kept private from me. The other side of the room holds a loveseat and a coffee table. I never understood why he needed that in here but it wasn't my office so I didn't ask questions. I feel the weight of everyone waiting for me to step into the office so we can get started. It pushes me to finally take the step that will put me inside the one room in our house that I was never allowed to enter before Charlie's death.

Stepping into the office feels like breaking a barrier though there was none. Once in I head over to his desk. Pru comes to stand next to me as I look down at Charlie's chair. A giant leather monstrosity. I would never choose one like this. I push it back and take a seat. Memré and Natasha bring boxes in and set them on the coffee table. Devon watches me from the other side of the desk.

Pru sets a hand on my shoulder, "What do you want us to do?" she asks softly. I look around, "Could you all tackle the filing cabinets? I have no idea what is in them, let me know if you see anything I should deal with or that you think I should see." She nods and the three women tackle the files behind me, Devon grabs a couple boxes and begins taping the bottoms for them and me.

I start with opening the middle drawer of the desk. Mostly office supplies and such, also a couple credit cards I have never seen. I dump the office supplies into the box Devon set next to me and put the cards on the desk. Devon picks up the cards while I open up the left side bottom drawer.

My jaw drops, "Oh my gawd. I can't believe he had these! Why would he have so many?" I hear things hitting the floor but I can't look away from the train wreck in front of my eyes. The drawer is filled with condoms, lube, and gloves. Mostly condoms of all different kinds. Pru clears her throat, "At least there are gloves?" I look up at her and laughter bubbles up and out of me. Natasha joins in with me first, Memré and Pru start laughing too. Devon is left standing there looking at the four of us with more than a little trepidation.

I finally manage to bring myself under control and hand on chest I work on calming myself down before that edge of hysteria takes over. Reaching around most of what is in the drawer I pull out the box of gloves and snag a pair out of it. Slipping them on I begin grabbing bunches of condoms to drop into the box. "I feel like I should donate these..." Devon laughs, "Not sure there are places that take condom donations? Besides, who knows how old those are or if the packages are all still intact? Probably better to trash them. For the safety of anyone looking to use a condom."

I nod in agreement as I start on the bottles of lube. Strawberry, cherry, banana? We never used these in our sex life. "You know, we never used any of this. I don't want to think about why he needed flavored lube but I feel like going through this last bastion of his things is going to be an education for me." I drop the last of the lube into the box, "Devon, can you get me a new box? I don't want to stare at this."

He grabs the box and deposits it on the loveseat while I turn to the drawer on the right. Biting my lip I pull the drawer open as I shut my eyes. When it won't open any further I peek at it, opening one eye. Oh good! It looks like just more files! I pull out the first folder and begin flipping through it, looks like old letters. I don't recognize any of the names so I set it aside to look at later. Maybe his mom will want them. Another folder, this one is full of bank statements. "Whoa. That is a lot of money. Why is my name on an account I have never known about till now? I mean great, its a joint account and has a lot of money in it. But where did this come from? Memré, I think I might need your help here..."

The file contains statements from a few accounts that I have never seen but all of which I am joint holder. Memré holds her hand out for the file, I hand it over. There were a lot of zeros there. Memré asks, "What was Charlie doing all these years? Holy crap. Honey, you can buy whatever house you want. It doesn't matter if you sell this one or not."

I shake my head, "I can't believe we had all this. Wait, don't you have to sign things to be on an account?" Pru, standing by my right shoulder says, "Yes. You do. The banks are pretty persnickety about that. You can do everything online but you are eventually going to have to show up and sign a paper. Well, for most places." I look at the faces around me, "Who signed for me? Why did Charlie have someone that would sign for me? Guys, I don't have a good feeling about this..."

Memré sets the file down on the desk, "Ok, this puts a spin on the files we are going through. We are going to need to go back through the files we have already tossed and review to be sure there is nothing important contained in them. The one thing I know for sure is that everything leaves a trail. Usually in paper. If you aren't sure about the importance of a paper, pass it round so we can all judge. Strange pictures? Those stay. Any thing that looks even remotely out of place."

Looking directly at me she says, "When I get home I will start tracing his actions online." I cock my head toward the computer I am sitting in front of, "Why not go through his computer?" She looks at the monitor like it has just appeared there, "Well, that would be easier. Sure. Want me to do that while you work on the rest of the desk?"

For an answer I hop up out of the chair and step aside. Memré sits down at the desk and moves the mouse. His monitor lights up with a sign in screen. The sign in is just a button, no password or anything. Memré looks up at me and back to the monitor. She moves the mouse and clicks the button. His desktop picture is a woman bent over holding herself open for the picture taker. "Eww. Well, you can change that if you can't stand seeing it while you go through there Memré. I have no idea who that is but it isn't me." She nods and gets to work while I go back to the file drawer.

Sitting on the floor I pull out the whole stack of files. Devon comes to sit across from me. I really love that he isn't crowding me while I deal with this. It's a lot and I need some space. I flip open the top file and immediately flip it closed again, "Ok, this one goes over here." I set it to the side.

Devon looks at me with curiosity written on his face and I tell him, "It is all pictures and I don't feel like I can deal with that just yet." He nods, "Would you like me to go through them for you?" I sigh in relief, "Yes I would." I grab the file up and hand it over to him, "Don't throw anything away just yet, but maybe sort them? One pile for sex pictures and another for important looking things and maybe one for the stuff that doesn't fit in the other two categories."

He opens the file and his eyes go round, "I, uh, I see what you mean. And I see why you slapped the file closed right after opening it. Geez." I open the next file and it seems to be deeds. And my name is on some of these. But not all of them. I guess I still own the others too because inheritance. Oh."

I remember what Benjamin said, Charlie was at his office regularly making sure I was the only one that could inherit. What if he faked a power of attorney and has been signing for me all this time? Natasha nudges me with her foot, "Hey. Gonna share?" I look around at her, "Huh?"

She chuckles, "You started talking and then cut off when something occurred to you. Care to share with the rest of the class?" "Oh, yes! Sorry." I hold up the file in my hand, "It looks like deeds in here. I was thinking that because of inheritance I probably own the ones that aren't in my name too. And then I remembered what Benjamin, our lawyer, said. He told me that Charlie was at his office regularly making sure I was the only one that could inherit from him. And I thought it was about his shady ass parents but now... Well, who was signing for me? Was it him? Did he fake a power of attorney? Or did he have a someone faking me?"

Devon holds up a picture, "I think I have the answer to that." He brings the picture over and she looks a lot like me. It is a level of creepy that I am not at all prepared to see. I shudder, "Now we need to see if this chick has identification that she is running around with that makes her appear to be me or did he hang on to it. Maybe these files in front of me? Oh god, we have to find this guys." We all go back to work but now things are moving faster and with a lot less precision. I flip through the files before me as quickly as possible.

I find my birth certificate with the wrong year on it but no id. Or social. Those files finished I snatch the drawer they came from out of the desk entirely. Some things fly out of the side and hit the chair Memré sits in before falling to the floor. I set the drawer off to the side and breathe a sigh of relief as I pick up what flew out. Now in my hands are the forged drivers licenses, of which there are multiple copies along with a social security card. Each of the licenses has a different woman on it that resembles me.

Looking at the women on the licenses I ask out loud, "Charlie, what were you doing?" Memré looks down at me, "If his computer records are anything to judge by, I would say nothing good. Honey, I don't think you should stay here any longer than you absolutely have to and with the money in those accounts you don't have to stay anywhere you don't want to be. I think this week I am going to make some time to come over here, you and I got some work to do." Holding the cards to my chest I ask, "What do we need to do?"

She scoots the chair back to turn it and face me, "We need to transfer all this money, into a brand new account that only you have access to, we need to get your lawyer to handle these deeds, and we need to check with him about some legalities. We also need to do some searching to see if anyone else is out there using your identity."

My eyes just went round over the implications of all that she said, "Well, I kind of need to stay here for a little bit. I have it warded though and I think I could convince Devon to stay with me," I glance at him and he nods his agreement, "while I get the rest of this handled and buy a different house. I will move out of this one and just have it sold. Will that help you to feel better about my level of safety?"

15

"I can't believe we found so much I didn't know about. I thought Charlie was the most regular guy ever. There wasn't a clue that he was doing anything shady or out of the ordinary." I lay my head down on the table to wallow a bit. Devon is making me real food, he says pizza, booze, coffee and croissants do not feed a body properly. I figure I am not a growing girl anymore so my diet is fair game.

Self pity isn't really my thing so I head for the office and grab the box of things we have found. Dumping it on the table I start sorting things. Bank stuff over there, all the fake id stuff over here, letters and pictures in another stack. Deeds. I think deeds are relatively safe to go through. I begin to page through them, one at a time. "Devon, I own property all over town. This one," I wave a deed at him, "is a really ritzy gated neighborhood. This one is near a library. This one is over near Pru, Memré, and Natasha. And this is…"

Devon turns from the dinner he is preparing as I drift off. I look back up at him, "This is a rental management contract. I am renting properties out to people." His brows raise and he turns back to the food he is cooking. "I need to call Benjamin. I am going to get him to come see this because this is just crazy." Devon's movements are tight, like he is annoyed.

Let me check on that before I call a human in here with the vampire. "Hey, are you ok? You look upset." His shoulders slump, "I am upset. But not with you or anyone else living. I am upset with myself and Charlie. Call Benjamin, he will be safe from me and you need this to be finished so you can move on."

"I see. Listen, you can't keep beating yourself up over this. I might have done the same thing if our positions were reversed." He grunts and carries on with the food so I just let it go. Setting down the deeds and contract I head for the bedroom and my cell. I call Benjamin on my way back to the table. "Hi Ben. Yes, I am doing great. But hey, I found some things that are really concerning in Charlie's office. Could you make a house call?"

The line is silent for a moment before he replies, "You know I don't do house calls right?" I nod, "Yes, I know. But I really need you to make an exception today. If I am right about the things I found, well, I can certainly give you a Christmas bonus this year." Silence again, "What did you find?"

"I found a lot of things Ben, I need you to come help me sort through this. I promise, it is not a wild goose chase. But I don't want to talk about it over the phone. Please, will you come?"

I hear him sigh, "I wouldn't do this for anyone else Fate. I have other clients and a home life. But, since you are also a good friend I will make an exception this time. I will be there in ten minutes."

"Thank you Ben, you won't regret it."

We end the call and Devon turns around with a plate of food for me. I elect to eat leaning against a counter and with a shrug, he does the same. He made me greens sautéed in bacon fat, roasted sweet potatoes, and shrimp also sautéed in bacon fat. It tastes so great and I didn't even know there was bacon or bacon fat here.

Really I think he could have made me a plate of gummy worms and it would have been delicious because someone else made it for me. We are both in deep thought while we eat. He eats quickly and starts cleaning what little mess remains. I finish eating as he wipes the last counter and he takes my plate, popping it into the dishwasher with the rest of the dishes.

Dropping the cloth onto the ledge in front of the sink he reaches over and pulls me into his big, strong arms. I press my face to his chest for a brief moment as I inhale his scent, old books and patchouli. I turn my face to the side as I slip my arms around him. He rubs my back as he holds me close. I have never felt so cared for in my entire life. I soak it up like it is the last rays of the sun on a cool day and it nourishes something deep within me that I didn't know was starving. We stand there until the bell rings and Devon releases me. I kiss his cheek and go let Benjamin into the house.

Benjamin has brought his briefcase with him and I thank him again for coming over like this. He looks annoyed but nods, "So where are these things you found?"

"Over here on the table, it is really a lot more than I would have ever dreamed would be hidden in that office and I am not sure we are done yet." I sit in the chair in front of the deeds and he takes the seat to the right of me. I don't see Devon anywhere and that is strange. I was going to introduce him, maybe he isn't comfortable with that. "Ok Ben, first," I reach over and grab the fake id's, "I found these in his office. I have someone checking into whether my identity has been further stolen." Ben's eyes get real big looking at the fakes, he keeps looking at me and back to the fakes. Ben clears his throat, "These are good. I can tell it isn't you but I don't think anyone that doesn't know you well could tell the difference."

"I know. That is part of what scares me. But wait, there's more." I reach for the bank statements and this time his jaw drops, "Holy shit Fate. I guess you can give me a Christmas bonus, can't you? Where did he get all this?" Shrugging I pick up the deeds and contract, "I have no idea. My guru is working on that too. Now, um, it would seem I own a good deal of properties here and I have a rental management company working for me as well."

Ben begins flipping through the deeds, "That's my office. You own my office? Ok Fate, I am sorry I doubted you. Holy shit." He runs a hand through his perfectly coiffed hair sending it spiking in all directions. I have never seen him so flustered. "Fate, do you have any idea what he did to get this? I mean, was he laundering money? I know he was an investment banker and that is a lucrative job most of the time, but this? This is so far out of the realm of what he should have based on what I know of his finances..."

"I know Ben, I don't know where it came from either. I have a stack of letters over here that I hope will give me a clue but nothing else. Yet." Ben stops flipping through deeds and looks at me, "What do you mean, you have a stack of letters? May I see them?" Reaching over the table I grab the last stack of paper on the table that he hasn't seen, "Sure. I have no idea what's in them. I haven't been able to bring myself to read them yet." Setting the deeds and contract aside he takes the stack of letters from me. I watch as he reads and grows more pale with each letter.

Finishing the letters Ben sets them carefully on the table, "Fate, these letters are to and from Charlie. I really think you need to read them and then put them in a safe deposit box somewhere. They are not addressed to you, but he kept copies for a reason. I cannot begin to guess at the reason. I don't think I even want to know honestly. I can take the deeds, the management contract; these things I can take care of for you. Did you say you have someone handling the accounts?"

"Mmmhmm, I do. She is a professional hacker but is doing this for me because we have known each other for so long. She will erase the trail as far as is possible too. No one that isn't at least as capable as her will be able to follow it."

"Good, good. Have her check out Charlie as well. If you find more properties, give me a call. As I said, I will get these," he holds up the stack of deeds and contract, "into just your name and make sure that any future monies go to you. I highly suggest that you close your current account and open a new one. At the same bank is fine, but you should have an entirely new account. Not just a new card. May I use one of the folders there to keep these separate?"

I nod as I hand over a folder and watch him place the stack he has been holding into the folder and then his briefcase. "I don't think you need to hear this but I won't sleep if I don't say it Fate. Be very cautious about allowing new people into your life. Especially people that come around saying they knew Charlie. He was," Ben gestures at the letters, "doing things that likely skated the edges of being legal and definitely involved dangerous people." He looks away for a second, "And Fate, Charlie had plans for you. Whether or not you read the letters is up to you but I don't know how far he got in setting those plans into motion before he died. Use the utmost in caution and beware new people, or even old friends of his. One more thing. Move. Don't stay in this house any longer than you absolutely have to, I don't think it is a safe place for you."

Sigh, "Thanks Ben. I will be more cautious. Before you go though, I want you to meet Devon. He is an old friend of mine, we had lost touch for a long time but he started a research project at my library. We started dating recently. He has been here the whole time but he didn't want to intrude." Ben looks suspicious as I raise my voice like Devon can't hear me just fine, "Devon! Can you come out here please?" We hear the bedroom door at the far end of the house open and Devon comes walking down the hall. "Devon, I would like you to meet Benjamin Smith. Ben, this is Devon. Devon Kordell."

Ben's eyes go wide again as he stands to shake Devon's hand, "The Devon Kordell? The Devon that is a brilliant lawyer? That Devon Kordell?" My jaw drops as Ben fawns over Devon, who is now blushing! Devon nods, "Yes, that is me. I wasn't planning to make it known that I am researching here for a while. Can you keep it quiet? I feel like it would draw unwanted attention to Fate right now. We both know that not all people practicing law are necessarily concerned with obeying it."

Ben shakes his head in agreement, "I feel so much better knowing that you are who she is seeing. I am very concerned after what I read in those letters. Charlie was not the person we thought he was and the people he was associating with are worse. Will you be staying with her until she leaves here, I hope?"

Devon looks to me and I nod, "It looks like I will Mr. Smith—"

"Please, call me Ben, if you are going to be in Fate's life we will run into each other. No need to stand on ceremony."

Devon smiles, "Only if you will call me Devon." Ben nods his agreement as Devon continues, "I will be staying with Fate until she moves out of this house." He looks over at me, "Unless maybe you would like to come stay with me while we get your affairs sorted and you decide where you would like to live?"

My mouth is hanging open, "I uh, that idea had not crossed my mind. But I like it. I think once we get this office finished we could do that. I can send people to pack things and put them in storage for me. Maybe we can go tomorrow. I will call Natasha later and ask for a night off to get this done. And we can get gone from here."

Both men look pleased with my decision. I don't need their approval but it is nice to have their support while I deal with all this. Ben fawns over Devon a little more on his way to the door, I follow behind the two of them completely entertained. I watch as Devon opens the door so that he can check before allowing anyone through it and he walks out ahead of Ben still looking around. I wait in the doorway, I don't need to listen to their chatter. Ben makes it into his car and backs out before Devon returns to the house.

"I guess you're moving in with me."

I laugh, "It looks that way. So where do you live anyway?"

He looks back at me, "I never told you where I live? Huh. I must have forgotten. I have a place in the Old North Durham area, it is an older neighborhood, parts are very upscale and old money. Other parts not so much.They think I am the youngest son of an old family. Really, the family is just me but I go away periodically and pass it down to an heir every so often. It is pretty gothic looking. And also really big. You could have your own room if you wanted, and an office if you like."

He looks really nervous now and I am guessing that would be due to his being polite enough to offer me a separate bedroom but not really wanting me to take him up on that offer. "So you would be okay with it if I wanted my own bedroom and didn't sleep next to you every night?" I can't help but mess with him after he gave me that opening. His shoulders droop for a moment but he tells me that would be fine, it is whatever I want. I laugh, "I want to sleep next to you! No way are you giving me my own bedroom. I wouldn't mind an office though."

I laugh more when he says all bright and cheered, "You can have any room you want for an office. We can get you furniture or some of the rooms have desks in them." He sounds so eager and he is being so sweet to me. I don't know what to do with all this kindness.

"Let's get everything out of the office and go through it out in the kitchen area where the table is. His office and the chair just creep me out now. Actually, my darling vampire, with all that boundless energy and strength, how about you carry all the files out here while I sort through them all. I think it might be the most efficient way to get this done." He nods and heads for the office while I go to the table. I collect up all that is still laying on the table, settling it carefully in the box that is marked 'TO KEEP'.

Devon brings the first armload of papers out of the office and so begins a night full of sorting my dead husband's life out. His shadow life is equal parts horrifying and mystifying. I don't understand how I could have not seen. The only thing I can come up with is that I just didn't care enough to wonder what he was doing. Nothing in my life mattered a whole lot beyond my sister and my friends. I know it crossed my mind that he might be sleeping around on me but I didn't care enough to follow up on it.

We seemed all right and I know there wasn't the slightest clue that he might want me dead. Why wouldn't he just divorce me? Why do men just jump straight to I have to kill her when they want to move on? Are they incapable of being honest enough to just divorce someone? I would much rather a divorce than a death. I certainly would never move from I want to be alone or with someone else to I guess my spouse has to die. I suppose it would be tidy for him as well as garnering him loads of sympathy.

I look up from the pile I have been sorting and see that Devon is sitting next to me just watching as I sort through the files lost in thought. That is probably the most considerate thing anyone has ever done for me, waiting while I finish a thought. He asks, "How are you holding up?"

"I think I am doing good. I want to go to the cemetery and curse my dead husband some more but I think that is a reasonable reaction all things considered. There is a lot of stuff in here, I can't even begin to understand how he didn't have an assistant to keep up with all this stuff. Maybe he did? I am so looking forward to Memré getting back here so we can start the process of moving the money from those accounts and into a whole new place."

I look around at the house, "And honestly, I am really ready to get out of this place. I don't want to be in the space we shared for so long any more. It feels tainted now that I have an idea of what he was doing." Devon presses his lips together, "It is pretty late, nearly 5. If you want to get some sleep before Memré comes back in a few hours, now is the time. Or we can stay up till you are ready to leave this place." He shrugs, "Either way."

I look at my watch in surprise, "I had no idea." I check the pile in front of me and look around for another one. The only piles of folders now are the one in front of me that I have been working my way through which has only three folders left and the piles I have sorted everything into. "I guess would you like to go through these with me and then we can get some sleep? It will finish out his office with the exception of the computer and Memré can print or email or put in dropbox whatever needs to be saved from that. Or a portable hard drive if she feels like it will be better to keep it offline."

Devon agrees and we make short work of the remaining files. Standing up I stretch and realize my whole body has protests over the treatment of the past few hours of work. "Ooooh, that hurts." I nearly drop back into the chair from the spasms, Devon catches my arms and helps me stay upright. "Thanks, being mortal is sometimes a bit of a pain." He looks over with a strange look on his face, "Maybe we could fix that..." I freeze, "What do you mean? Like, me be a vampire?"

"If you were inclined. I am not ever going to try to push you to it, but I wanted you to know that it could be an option if you chose." I flip off lights as we move toward the bedroom and he goes on to say, "I didn't think it would be something that had occurred to you yet and maybe it is something you would want to consider. The one that has killed you in every other lifetime is a vampire, and that is probably why you have never seen his face. I mean, there are some benefits. But, I don't know what it would take from you. I need to talk to Malachi."

I close the bedroom door behind us, "Well, I won't rule it out. I do need more information. Will I still be a witch? Does it hurt a witch to become a vampire? Are there any rules against it? Do you all have a governing body? I know witches don't but you vampires live a lot longer and maybe you have one?"

Devon laughs, "Some of those I don't know the

answer to, after my friend Billy gets here we will work on getting in touch with Malachi, he is the oldest of us. He is more likely to have the answers we need for you than anyone else I know. For now, you need sleep love." I walk over to him, "I do need sleep, but I need you first." He grins as we come together and he guides us into the bed.

16

I wake to the sound of Devon talking to Memré at the door to the bedroom. I am not quite ready to focus on anything except his naked butt, he has his body angled so it is behind the door and not flashing his whole package at Memré, I am sure that she really appreciates that. Or maybe not! Ha!

They finish talking and he closes the door. I grin as he turns around and I do get to see his whole package. What a nice package it is too. He notices my grin and shakes his hips so his dick slaps each thigh a couple times before he laughs and dives onto the bed over me.

I am giggling over the show, he pretends to pout. "You laughing at me? I think my manhood is insulted." I laugh harder and push him off me, "I have to pee now mister, you're killin' me." I freeze, "Wait, do you still pee? Is it the same as the rest of us? Oooo, is it red?" He rolls his eyes at me, "Yes I still pee, yes it is the same as it was before I was turned, I don't want to know why you thought it might be red. Go, make your bathroom trip."

He chuckles, "Memré is waiting for us out there and she is making coffee." I make my bathroom visit and come back out refreshed, with my teeth brushed too.

I step over to the closet and grab some yoga pants and a t-shirt. I throw them on and stepping out of the closet I see my bra on the floor, do I want to bother with it? Nah. Devon steps out of the bathroom and grabs his pants, I stop to watch him put them on. He smirks at me as he buttons them. I walk over and grab his shirt from a different spot on the floor, tossing it over to him. I open the door to the aroma of coffee filling the house and I follow my nose to the kitchen. Memré turns and hands me a full cup as I draw near. I take that first beautiful sip as she says, "Looks like you were seriously busy last night."

"Yeah, I got Benjamin to come by too. He has the deeds and stuff. Apparently I own his office building. He will be filing things and making sure everything is properly transferred to me. The accounts, we get to handle that. He read the letters and says I should read them too. I am not at all ready for that. He also 'suggested' that I not stay here. So today the plan is that we get everything taken care of with his computer and the accounts." Memré nods, "And once that is done I will pack a little bag and take myself along with some important items over to Devon's house."

Her eyes bug a little but she manages to swallow her

coffee without choking. "Devon's house?" She looks over at Devon as he sips his coffee leaning against the counter near me. I sip more of the sweet nectar that is my morning coffee and I tell her, "Yes. I don't know if we will stay there permanently but I don't feel weird living with him so quick, we have lived together before. It isn't like we just met, I know tons about him. His favorite color is green, he doesn't know how to relax, you could literally bounce a quarter off that ass..."

Devon looks over at me in surprise, I laugh. "Yes, I remember doing that and even though it wasn't a quarter back then I figure it is about equivalent size." Memré giggles into her coffee, and swallowing first she says, "I guess it just takes some getting used to for us. We did just meet him and until recently you didn't remember him. He was just that guy at the library bugging you and making you super hot and bothered." I look over my shoulder at Devon smirking into his coffee, "Yeah, he is still making me hot and bothered but now he gets to do something about it."

Memré laughs at me, "You ready to do this thing? I don't need to hear about your fantastic sex life while I am in this drought. We need to get the account stuff situated first and then you can get things sorted to take with you to Devon's." She looks at the two of us, "As strange as this whole situation is I am really glad you won't be staying here after today. I am also really glad you will be with Devon and that he will be working to keep you safe."

Devon says, "Me too Memré, me too."

"Oh crap, I need to call Natasha and tell her I need tonight off. Let me go do that real quick and then I will meet you in the office, ok?"

"Sure, see you in there."

A FEW MINUTES later I step into the office, Memré has his computer booted up and ready. She also has her laptop sitting open on his desk. I look at the set-up and then her, she answers my unspoken question, "I am going to use his computer to take care of the things on his end and mine to take care of things on your end. I don't know what he might have hooked to his so I don't want to put any of your information in his computer. I set up two accounts for you last night. One is offshore, the bulk of your money will be there and the other is local. After I get everything transferred to the offshore account I will put a few hundred thousand into the local one. You will only need to stop by there and sign the papers to pick up your cards. The offshore account will not require an in person visit. But they will mail you things to sign. So I will need an address for that. And for the accounts in general. But then you will be all set and have a ridiculous amount of money at your disposal."

"She already does."

We both turn to look at Devon, "What do you mean I

already do?" He shrugs, "I have money and you are welcome to anything I have so therefore you have a ridiculous amount of money at your disposal." Memré and I share a look, sigh and shake our heads.

She turns back to her work and I explain to Devon, "That is not how it works. I appreciate that you feel that way but your money is yours and I am not comfortable depending on you. That is a large part of the reason why I kept working while Charlie was alive. I need to have my own money. I don't and won't spend my life dependent on someone else. If I decided to walk away from you I would not still have access to all your money, right? Right."

He opens his mouth to say something and I hold my hand up, "Nope. That cannot be guaranteed. You might be mad and decide I can kick rocks for all you care. Or you might be incapacitated. What then? I should have my own money and that is how it will be. Always."

Devon presses his lips together, brows drawn down. I wait while he turns this over in his mind, I have faith that he will understand given a minute. Finally he nods and says, "I see what you mean. What I said sounded as though I intended that you be dependent on me. I wouldn't want that for you. I do want you to know I am here for you if you are ever in need or are willing to let me spoil you." He grins with that last bit and I walk over to kiss him, he is just so damn cute.

A few kisses later Memré is telling us, "Ugh. Do that later. We need to do things here. I need an address and for you to give me info to do these accounts." After one last kiss Devon says, "Let me write the address down for you and then I will go load the cars with the boxes of paperwork." I drag a chair in while he writes down his address. He cups my cheek briefly on his way out of the room. I get myself seated and Memré gets us to work.

AN HOUR and a half later we have everything sorted. I have two new accounts, a paper with the info written on it as well as a picture of the info on my phone. Memré hands me a portable hard drive, "This has everything that was on this computer, in case you need something from it one day. Now, we need to power it off and do some destruction."

She smiles in glee with the idea of destroying the dinosaur of a computer that Charlie insisted was the best ever. He always acted like upgrading it was a Greek tragedy. I didn't care since I have a laptop of my own that I haven't used a whole lot until now. Now I think I may have no choice but to use it a lot more. Once the computer is powered down she starts disconnecting it from all its wires.

"Do you have a screwdriver and a hammer?" I nod and head down the hall to the laundry room. I dig in a cabinet and pull out a phillips and a flathead along with a 20 ounce hammer. Back in Charlie's office Memré looks at what I brought and takes the phillips screwdriver from me. She makes quick work of taking the side panel off the computer. Reaching in she pulls out a couple memory sticks.

She sets those on the desk with the screwdriver. Then, taking the hammer from me, with great enjoyment she bashes the motherboard into tiny bits. It takes some doing since there is not much space in the case but she is very thorough. None of the motherboard remains attached to the case when she finishes. She grabs the waste basket and dumps all the pieces into it. Snapping the memory sticks into a few pieces and they get tossed in as well.

That done she pulls the bag out and ties it up before holding it out to me, "Take this with you and throw it in a landfill somewhere. It probably can't be put back together but who knows. These dinosaurs were really tough and would survive a lot." I take the bag, "Sure thing. I guess you have things to do now?" I ask as she works at closing her computer and putting away all her gear. She nods, "Yeah, I have some errands to run, but this was important."

I walk her out, chatting with her about normal things that make us both feel more grounded. I hug her before she leaves, "Thank you, I don't know what I would do without you." She smiles, "I know. You need me. Helpless without my awesomeness." She laughs and puts her bags in the car, "Love you, stay safe."

I WATCH her drive off and turn to go pack my bags. Devon is standing right behind me, I scream and lash out with air, pinning him to the wall across the room. He laughs, "Good reflexes, want to let me down now?" I let him down as I kick the door shut, hand on my heart because it is still trying to beat right out of my chest. He strolls toward me, all casual. Maybe I should pin him to the wall and leave him there for a while.

He smiles like he knows what I am thinking, I imagine it probably shows on my face. "So, Fate, that reaction was perfect. If you do it to someone that doesn't know about magic then just spell them to forget it. But if you have done it to a vampire or a stalker, don't let them go and call me. I packed your clothes and all your jewelry and toiletries. You two took a very long time and I didn't want to disturb you. Is there anything else you need?"

Walking off toward the bedroom I say "Yes, I need my altar box and some papers I have stashed. Did you already load what you packed?"

"Of course." He grabs my purse off the dresser, "Do you need the trash bag from the office?"

"Yes. And the notes on the desk. Do you have coffee at your place?" He nods and heads to the office for the bag and the notes. We meet up outside, I see that both cars have boxes lining the back seat. He was a busy man while we worked. Devon hands over my purse and gives me a quick kiss, "Following me or gps-ing it?"

"GPS I think, I have it on my phone and I need to know the way there. It is easier for me to remember it if I drive with the lady in the box telling me so I can look at landmarks and street signs." He laughs and gets in his car. I get in mine and wait as he pulls away. As I look one last time at the house I spent so much time not living in, I wave my hand to dissipate the warding. Pulling out of the driveway I know I will never see this house again.

17

Twenty minutes later I arrive at Devon's house. It is gorgeous. Dark blue, almost purple trim accents the slate gray of the house. The door is a vibrant purple. I open the car door and stand there just looking at the yard. It is a witch's dream.

There are big, bushy herbs growing all over the place. I grab my purse and head for the door. I hit the button to lock my car as I go, I didn't see anyone follow me but who knows. As I reach the door Devon opens it, "Welcome home, would you like the grand tour?" He looks so excited to have me there, I can't say no. "Yes, this place is lovely. How long have you had it?"

"Oh, about a hundred years. The gardens I had started about fifty years ago. The inside I had done around twenty years after I got the place. It was very colonial before that." He leads me into the first room off the entry, "This was originally a salon, it still is to some extent but there is a desk over there." We go through a few other rooms before we get to the kitchen and what a kitchen it is! It is huge, with an island creating a walkway between it and the counter space.

The stove is a large professional model with a Viking vent over it. The refrigerator is enormous. I open it and find it well stocked, "You eat all this? I thought you did more drinking than actual eating of food?"

"I do a lot of drinking though I also eat frequently. But, as I knew you were coming here I had my house-keeper stock the kitchen so you wouldn't have to worry about it."

Sweet Lady, the man is a saint. I follow him out of the kitchen and up the stairs, the first room he shows me has a large dark wood desk with scroll work along the edges and an ergonomic chair in a blue violet color pushed up to it. Along the far wall is a couch with a small table at either end. A large peace lily graces a corner. The walls are a pale purple with slate accents and I love it. "This one. This is the office I want. Unless," I look over at him, "is this your office?"

"No, this office has always been waiting for its owner. I hoped you would like it. I didn't know if you would ever be here but I always try to make a spot that will be for you."

Turning slowly so I can take it all in, "Well spot on good sir, I love this room. This is my ideal office and I don't know if I will ever leave here." As I stop my turning to face him I see he is smiling softly as he watches me. "You've been waiting for me for a long time, haven't you?"

His eyes grow sad as he answers, "I have, but only because I couldn't protect you well enough before. I should have kept you safe."

I walk to him and put my arms around him, "It isn't your fault that some jerkface keeps killing me. I mean honestly, what kind of person does that? Wait, it's a vampire isn't it?" He nods, "Oh, that explains a lot. Well, still. It is a sign of derangement on his part. You are not to blame. We will be extra cautious this time and work hard to keep me alive. I am older and more experienced this time around too, plus I am way more sick of everyone's shit than I was as a younger woman. We will make it through this."

He smiles but it never reaches his eyes, "Come, I know you must be tired by now. It has been a long day. I want to show you our bedroom."

Four doors down the hall and he opens one on the opposite side of the hall, it takes my breath away. Dark wood everywhere, all the furniture is this dark, old wood that shines with the gloss of loving care.

The bed is a sleigh style with deep blue bedding. The walls are a blue gray color and there is a huge fire place off to one side of the room. I see a door for a closet and another that likely holds a bathroom but all I want to do is see how soft this bed is and is it actually possible to fall asleep when your head touches the pillow?

I stand next to the bed and kick off my shoes, I look

over to Devon still standing in the doorway, "Is there anyone else here?"

He shakes his head no, watching me like he is in a daze. I need to be in this bed right now, so I figure whatever it is will hold for a few minutes. I shove my pants down over my hips and pull my feet out as I snatch my shirt up and over my head. Clothes shucked I slowly pull the covers back and climb into the bed. It is so soft, the sheets are divine and I am in heaven. Maybe that guy killed me already and I am in heaven with Devon. Huh, that rhymes. "Devon?"

He doesn't respond but my voice seems to have broken his trance. One moment he is standing in the doorway fully clothed and the next he is naked on hands and knees over me, his eyes boring into mine and his pupils very large. "Um, Devon, are you okay?"

"Yes. I have wanted to see you in my bed for a very long time. You just granted that wish and you are so lovely and naked under these covers. I want you, and if you were willing to make love with me right now it would be a culmination of the many fantasies I have had laying alone in this bed wandering where you were."

I am deeply touched and now incredibly horny from that little speech so rather than answer him I grasp the top of the blanket and begin to reveal my body to him inch by slow inch. His eyes grow darker as he tracks the progress of the covers down my body.

I have never felt so sexy in my entire life as I do now pushing a blanket off my 40 year old body. He moves his hands as they begin to trap the blanket. When I get to the extent of my reach he moves to one side and whips the rest of the blanket down and off my body.

He is over me again, his cock so hard I can see veins throb in it. He leans down and begins trailing kisses along my neck and down my collar bone. His kisses flow to my left breast that is just begging to be in his mouth. He drops kisses in a circle around the nipple, finally taking it in his mouth, he makes me gasp with the pleasure of it.

He suckles hard, and I moan. He sets the nipple free from his mouth with a light pop. Before I can voice my disappointment he has the right nipple in his mouth and is sucking hard, I feel my core clench in ecstasy. I feel one of his hands lift from the bed but I don't care as long as he keeps that nipple in his mouth. Then I feel a finger slide between my very wet folds and begin to rub the pearl hidden there and suddenly I care a lot about that hand, moans tear out of me as he quickly sends me over the edge into the little death.

He releases my nipple from his mouth and nudges my legs further open with one knee. I am quite compliant right now and spread my legs wide for him. I feel him move his legs so he is between mine, then he lifts them and lines his cock up with my still spasming slit. As he slowly presses into my folds I die a little more. Every little press forward sends sparks running through my body lighting fires of pleasure that I have not felt without him.

Fully encased within my hot core he holds still, his

eyes closed. I want the tingles so I begin to rock my hips and he gasps, his entire body clenching. "Don't move, I don't want to finish yet." I laugh because I know he won't even get soft if he finishes now so I rock my hips slower but with much more exaggerated movements. He groans and sweats a little.

I rock downward so only the tip is still within my folds before I slam up to the hilt, he jerks and I feel him shooting inside me. I start to rock my pelvis and get a good rhythm going, his moans exciting me.

I watch as my core swallows his cock whole repeatedly and it turns me on even more. He moans and begins to pump in time with the rhythm I set, rocking his pelvis so it hits my pearl just right to send me off to orgasm land again. I feel him start to cum as my core clenches over and over around him.

Sweet Lady, how did I survive this long not having this delight?

He moves to the side and lays next to me, still breathing heavily. Breathing heavy myself I ask him, " I thought vampires didn't need to breathe? Why are you breathing heavy after that?"

"Because I haven't died. Vampires that die don't have to breathe, the ones that manage to stay alive still breathe, blood pumps through their veins, and they can eat regular food. The dead ones cannot take food anymore but alcoholic drinks are fine. No more coffee either. The bonus is they can also have sex and never get winded." He shrugs, "There are trade-offs for each. I prefer to live for as long as possible. I feel like it would be odd not breathing and I would miss food."

18

I wake up late the next morning, feeling delicious. I slept better last night than I have ever slept in my life. This bed is the best and I was tired in all the right ways when I went to sleep last night. I pick up Devon's arm from my waist and bring his hand up to kiss the palm then set it down next to me. Devon stirs a bit but doesn't really wake up.

I slide to the edge of the bed and sit up with my legs dangling over the edge. I stretch and move before hopping lightly down to the floor. Padding quietly over to the doors on the far wall, the first one I open is closet. Man is it huge. I could fit a whole room in there.

What I need though is a bathroom so I move on to the next door. Opening that one is like finding a spa operates in your house. The windows keep it well lit, plus they appear to have a film on them for added privacy. The counter seems to go on forever and has two raised sinks with waterfall spouts hanging over them.

I see no toilet but there is a door on the far side of the room, I head for that and find exactly what I am looking for. Emerging a few minutes later feeling very refreshed, I go back to the bedroom to put on my clothes from last night. I grab my phone from my purse and head downstairs toward that gorgeous kitchen.

There is a message from Natasha, she says that I should take a second night off. She doesn't want me overworked with all that is going on and Anelle says she needs the hours anyway. Plus, Charles the creeper was very rude to Anelle when she wouldn't tell him when I would be back to work and now Anelle's boyfriend Roger the security guard will be hanging out tonight.

They are adorable and I love that Anelle has him. I find him pretty boring to talk to but I don't have to date him so it's all good. I text her back that I am great with that idea. Stepping into the kitchen I start opening cabinets looking for the coffee. I finally find it, ten cabinets in. Whole beans and no grinder in the same cabinet. If I were a grinder where would I be hiding?

Hmm, the coffee was mid-kitchen so let's check the far end. Of course, there it is. What sadist set up this kitchen? At least the coffee maker is out in the open. I get the coffee started and begin a search for a cup. Sure, I could drink it straight from the pot but it seems a little dangerous with my lack of coordination first thing in the morning. Cups, cups, where are they? Ah, down in a bottom cabinet. Why the fuck would they be there? Devon and I are really going to have to have a talk about this kitchen.

It is bananas.

What kind of people live like this? I wonder if he has ever even made his coffee here. I finally get my coffee put together and sit down at the island to sip and scroll my social media. I hear someone shuffling in and I look over to the doorway, my eyes nearly pop out of my head. This woman is a walking embodiment of Trunchbull only smaller. She glares at me, looks at the coffee pot and says, "What are you doing? Who told you that you could make coffee? Who let you in?"

I cannot believe this woman. Benefit of the doubt, maybe she is morning cranky too. "I told me that I could make coffee. I live here now, my name is Fate. You are?"

Her face twists like she was fed a live worm, "I am none of your business is what I am. Where is Mr. Kordell?"

"I see. Well, *ma-Damn*, figure it out yourself. I have coffee to drink. If I wanted to deal with rude I would go see creepy man. He at least has enough manners to carry a conversation."

"How dare you! Insolent creature! I should—"

"Watch your tongue before I turn Fate loose on you?" Devon had come down while we conversed and was now leaning on the door frame at the entrance to the kitchen, shirtless with pajama pants riding low on his hips. Sweet

Lady he is hawt. The worm lady got so pale when he spoke that I am a little worried she is going to pass out. Probably be a mess when she cracks her skull on the tile.

"Sir, I was just asking where you might be. Fate... was less than forthcoming." Wow. I never knew what people meant when they said someone spit their name out like it tasted foul until now. Her voice did a one-eighty talking to him too. I wonder if she is some sort of mythical shape-changing creature?

Devon raises an eyebrow at her, "I heard the entire conversation Maude. You were rude from the minute you walked in. This house has always been for Fate, she is mistress of it whether she is here or not. You are hired help, well paid but hired. If you cannot treat her with courtesy and respect then you will leave." He walks toward me and it is all I can do not to drool. I manage it by taking a sip of my coffee. Her wormliness watches with her jaw dropped in indignation at the lecture she was just given. Devon slips an arm around me and kisses the top of my head, "How's your morning love?"

Wormina spins on her heel and leaves the room in a huff. "Is Maude a former lover? Wow is she possessive. What is her deal?"

Devon chuckles, "No. I haven't had any lovers any of the times you were gone. I simply wasn't interested. Maude has only been here a few years, I think you are the first person she has ever seen here that isn't me. I switch out house help every few years to keep them from noticing how little I age."

I shrug, "That makes sense. I am so sorry that you have spent so much time waiting for me. Alone. Maybe we should look into getting this thing lifted?"

I feel him stiffen, he leans back and touches my chin to lift my face, "Fate, I want you to listen really close. I do not regret a minute of the waiting. The only thing I regret a little is that I waited this time. I should have come to find you much sooner. I don't want this gone, if it could ever be lifted. It can't and that was why it was such a hard thing to attain. It is forever. In addition, when we originally did this we planned for you to become like me. The witches we worked with fully supported this because they wanted you to carry the lore down through the ages. As it is, I have kept it for them. I have stayed in contact with those families and they have made copies of their pages to update the books I have as needed. If they lost a book for some reason, fire or flood or tornado, they still had the ones I hold as backup."

Now I am the idiot with a jaw hanging open. "I need a minute to process all this. Sit so I don't get a kink in my neck."

"One moment love, I would like some coffee too. Would you like a second cup? Perhaps an Irish cup to fortify your nerves?"

"Yes. Yes, I would like an Irish cup. That would be great and would definitely help me as I wrap my head around things."

He makes quick work of getting the coffee ready while I finish the cup I have. I was planning to become a vampire? I mean, it does have its merits. I would be more difficult to kill. But would I lose my witchyness? I don't know if I am willing to give that up. I am so deep in my thoughts that it startles me when he slides the cup in front of me.

"You know, you could probably pull up the memories yourself. You have them, and I don't think it would be difficult if you focused on what you wanted to remember. Might be easier even if you had a little of the coffee before you give it a go."

"I could, couldn't I? This is all so new, I still forget I have all that in there." I sip the coffee he made for me, oh the man knows what he is doing with the coffee. I love it. A couple more sips and I feel less frazzled and more able to focus. I set the cup down and close my eyes, picturing myself wandering through the vaults of my mind.

I see the memories as books that when opened to different pages will play different memories. My intuition guides me to a particular book, it is a deep green leather cover and thick. I pull it out and hold it in front of me still closed till I feel where to open it to for the memory I am seeking.

I open the book and I see a group of witches before me. We are discussing the lore-keeping and the role I could play. I asked them the same questions then, would I lose my power if I became vampire? One of the witches told me no, that a sister had been a vampire and was performing the job I would be taking on until the witch trials got her.

She was tortured to death but never revealed anything to them. The conversation went on, talking about the role I would play and how my longevity would be a boon to all witches. Watching this memory brought tears to my eyes, I could feel them running down the face in my mind and my physical face, it brought me out of my mind and I watched as the book floated back into place while I returned to my body. I open my eyes to find Devon watching me with concern written across his face.

I wipe my face, "Oh Devon, I've missed so much! The guy that killed me stole so much from so many people that were depending on me." Fresh tears run down my face and I find I just don't even care. Movement in the doorway brings both of our attention to the worm queen walking into the kitchen. She manages to ratchet her neck up a little bit further and look down at me. I look at Devon, lips pursed and brows raised. He nods, worm-lady has to go.

"Well, I need a shower now," I sip the coffee but it is cold and foul now. "Would you bring my clothes in? I don't have the slightest idea where you packed everything."

Devon chuckles, "I will bring it all in. Are your keys laying out where I can find them?"

"They're in my purse. Dive in, it's all good. I don't have anything bite-y in there today." I grin at him as I leave the room heading for the glorious shower I know awaits me in that bathroom upstairs.

AN HOUR later I am showered and feeling more put together. I don't know if he still wants me to be vampire but the longer I think about it the more I want to take on the duty that I had planned to take on so long ago. I need to talk to Devon about it, but later. For now, I missed a call from Benjamin. I hit the button to call him back, he picks up after the first ring.

"Hi Benjamin, how are things going for you?"

"Well, the property manager is frankly, not someone that I would ever choose to work with."

"Oh, what is he doing? What will this affect?"

"He is insisting that you come in person to sign new contracts as the previous ones were with your husband. He wants me to believe that he is within his rights to withhold payments and keep them permanently. He is not and I will sue his company into the ground if he tries it. But, I think you should meet with him, with Devon and I both present. I also suggest that you seriously consider a different management company. Though I suppose it is within the realm of possibility that he will behave better after we meet with him in person."

"I see. Ok, call him back and set up an appointment for this afternoon. I am not working tonight so I have time. I may drop back to part time anyway. Text me when the appointment is and the address. Devon and I will meet you there."

Benjamin agreed and we ended the call so he could

handle this property manager. Good grief. What a pain. I shove my phone into my back pocket and start out of the room when I hear yelling. Oooh, it's wormessa! I peek around the door, can't see the entry from here so I creep out and down the hall a bit, she is really pissed.

I wonder if she is part banshee? Man, I have never heard so many uncomplimentary words in reference to myself from someone I haven't even had sex with. I'm kind of impressed honestly. I get to the top of the stairs and I see her storming off toward the door and I just hang out watching, I have seen movies with less action than this lady screaming like a banshee with a gift for obscenity.

She opens the door and turns back to scream at Devon that my money grubbing ass will have him in the poorhouse in no time. I can't help myself, I start laughing. Concerned that I might roll my own ass down the stairs I sit and just keep laughing, long and loud. She is creative, but so far off base. She hears me and looks up at me, gives me the finger and slams the door on her way out. I just laugh harder.

When I finally manage to collect myself Devon is at the bottom of the stairs, arms crossed in front of his chest and watching me with a smirk. "Oh goodness, I am sorry Devon. I wasn't going to reveal my presence up here until she started with the money grubbing bit. Then I couldn't do anything but laugh. It just bubbled up and out. Her flipping me off made it even better. I am really impressed with her creativity though. I might have to try some of the things she suggested I was doing for pay."

The last bit cracked him and Devon started laughing. Catching my breath I ask him, "So. Mister Vampire, want to run up here and let me tell you my news without shouting?" Still laughing he climbs the stairs and comes to sit next to me on the top step. "Benjamin called and the," my phone dings with multiple messages. I look down and see they are from Benjamin so I go on, "property manager is a jerk. He insists I come and sign a new contract since the old one was between him and Charlie. I told Benjamin to get an appointment set for this afternoon. He, Benjamin, wants you to come as well. I think he wants to make it absolutely clear that I have plenty of male backup." Devon had gone from smiles and laughter to a very serious face while I spoke.

"Did he say anything else?"

"Only that he doesn't like the guy and he wants to cheat me out of current and future rent monies. Oh, and he strongly suggested that I look into a different property management company. I agree with that and plan to call Maggie. But, I still need to go meet with him. To collect keys if nothing else. I am going to keep Benjamin's firm hopping with all this work."

Devon is still very serious looking, I would probably be scared if I was anyone else. He nods his head and says, "I take it that is what the messages were about?"

. . .

"OH! YES, LET ME..." I open the messages from Benjamin and hold the phone so he can read them as well.

<He would prefer to talk to you over a late lunch. I told him you were unavailable for such appointments ever.>

<The appointment is set for 3 pm. He requested that you meet him alone, I vetoed that per our conversation. He is unhappy.>

<Would you like me to call Maggie? I think she does management as well.>

Devon's frown deepens. "I think you should dress up for this. I am going to wear a suit as well."

"Well, it looks like I am going to another funeral so I guess I can put on the pantsuit I wore to my cousin's funeral last year." Devon manages a chuckle for that.

I love making him laugh. I quickly text Benjamin back before I stand, telling him we will see him there and that I fully intend to call Maggie.

WE TOOK our time dressing and made sure we looked very serious and very uptight. Devon helped me put my hair in a bun. So serious. I feel like Kocoum today, as serious as we are behaving. Sounds like a great time to bring up the vampire thing with Devon. It might be easier to check in with the memories about how he feels but that might have changed since we originally planned it.

Oh. I might want to check in with Prudence about this too... Crap. Wait, she will be okay with this as soon as I explain it to her. She was already getting right with it anyway. I will talk to her before we make any permanent changes as a courtesy since she is my sister.

I wait till we are in his car on our way to meet sir dickbag to bring up turning me. "I have been thinking. Maybe we should do the turning me into a vampire thing."

Devon is silent for long minutes, "I would love knowing that you have the multiple defenses that being a vampire and witch would give you, but I don't want to push you into making this decision. I would ask that you think long and hard—"

"If I think long and hard we are not making it to my appointment." I snicker as he rolls his eyes at me.

"As I was saying, I would like you to... spend more time thinking about this before we commit to anything. Especially since your sister had an issue with me being a vampire. I know she is important to you and I would not want to be the cause of that relationship breaking."

"I agree that I need to talk with my people before we do anything but I also wanted to get your take on it. See if you were still willing to do this. And, I would like to know more about it. I am sure I could check my memories but I think it would be quicker if you would just tell me."

He chuckles at my impatience, "I would be happy to discuss it with you but we are here, and there is Benjamin. Raincheck?"

"Definitely."

We get out of the car and walk over to where Benjamin waits. The building is a squat brick place in decent repair, nothing special to call attention to it. We walk around the building to the front door, Benjamin opens the door and holds it while Devon and I pass through. The woman at the desk looks up at Devon and Benjamin, "Can I help you?"

Benjamin glances at me before he tells her, "Yes, Ms. Owens has an appointment with Anthony."

She rolls her eyes, "Have a seat." She waves in the direction of the lone chair the waiting room boasts. Eyeing the condition of the chair I opt to stand. Fifteen minutes later Anthony comes to the door and opens it to welcome me in, "Ms. Owens if you please." And he gestures into his dark office. Nah. I am not going down like that and my bodyguards are having none of it either.

Benjamin walks into the office first, I follow behind him and Devon brings up the rear. Stepping into the office we see he has candles lit and music playing. The kind of music a teenage boy with all his brains in his dick would play for his first sexual experience. Devon flips the light switch on as he passes it and I work very hard to keep a straight face.

Anthony shuts the door with more force than is necessary before walking over to stand behind his desk. Benjamin introduces myself and Devon. I decline to shake hands because I don't want to touch him, he looks like the kind of guy I would walk three blocks extra to avoid passing on a sunny day in a crowded public place.

There are only two chairs on this side of the desk so I take the one on the left, Benjamin the right, and Devon remains standing behind me. Sir Bag o'dicks starts talking about a ten percent fee and what that fee doesn't include. Seems like it would be quicker to tell us what he does do, which amounts to he will collect rents. Then he moves on to what is included with the twenty percent fee and I just stop him holding up my hand, "Wait, twenty percent? I mean, ten percent was ridiculous, and absolutely not happening."

I see Benjamin grinning out of the corner of my eye and it really just inspires me, "But then you decide I am completely ignorant of how things work or what a normal fee would be. It is amazing that anyone at all has been willing to work with you. I can't imagine Charlie agreeing to a deal such as this so I have to assume that you are tacking on an extra fee since we have messed up your plans for seduction here. FYI, I don't know who told you that music or that cologne were magnets for sex but they were wrong. I do believe that you could actually get in a lot of trouble for what you attempted here."

Both Devon and Benjamin nod, "So, here's the thing *Tony,* you are going to hand over the keys and leases to every piece of property that I own and we are going to walk out of here to go meet with the new property management team that I hired this morning." Benjamin is over there with this huge shit-eating grin directed at sir dickbag, and for his part the dickbag is very quiet and fuming. "Well, it will take some time to collect all-"

Devon cuts him off, "It will take all of five minutes to collect those things and we will be happy to wait right here while you get them. Or I can call an officer to aid us in collecting Ms. Owen's property?"

19

He is going to break his teeth gritting them like that. "That won't be necessary."

"Are you quite sure? I feel that they would love a reason to poke around in your office." Benjamin says with his grin finally put away. Sir dickbag negates that idea once again and begins to print lease copies while he pulls keys off a board that covers the top half of one wall. Ten minutes later everything is printed and a pile of keys sits on the desk in front of Benjamin.

Sir dickbag says, "I believe that is everything. Collect your things and get out."

My two guardians smirk as Benjamin sweeps the keys into his brief case while Devon collects and peruses the printed leases. Devon finishes going through the stack and nods at Benjamin and I before he hands them over to Benjamin. Benjamin leads the way out of the office while Devon brings up the rear again. I really doubt dickface is actually going to do anything beyond sit in his office and pout like the impotent jerk he is but I get the safety protocal.

Outside we head over to stand midway between the two cars and discuss the next step. Benjamin leads with "So, are we going to call the same one as I suggested to you before?"

"Yes, we will be meeting up with them shortly. I can sign and then they can meet with you to untangle all of this. In the meantime, can you see to getting locks changed for all the properties? I don't want him able to bother these people if he has more copies of the keys he gave you. He seems shadier than I really want to think about."

Nodding he says, "Yes. I agree. I will send a paralegal out with letters informing everyone of the changes as well as a locksmith to change all the locks."

"Wonderful. I really appreciate having you to count on with all this going on."

Benjamin and Devon shake hands as we part ways, Benjamin heading to his office and us to a meeting with Maggie the realtor.

WE MEET Maggie at a little café with great mediterranean food. I get to have this giant salad while Devon scarfs a beef-laden gyro and Maggie enjoys a regular sized salad. I take a sip of my water and begin telling her about the house and the plans I have now that I have come into this money. She offers to get it all set up for me and have the house staged so as it will sell faster. I love this idea and I tell her, "You are my new favorite person. Yes, please do all these things and send me bills. Thank you so much."

She shrugs, "This is what I do and honestly, this makes my job so much easier. You are quite sure you have everything you want out of that house, correct?"

"Yes, everything in there can be donated or go with the house or whatever. I haven't any personal effects left in the house. Just furniture and such. Food I wasn't eating anyway."

"Do whatever you think is best with it all and send me a bill. I just want to be done with that place. The others, well, I want them all inspected. Not for infractions on the part of the tenants but to see what should be taken care of and get it fixed. I don't want to even have a slight appearance of being a slum lord and I feel like my husband might have been exactly that."

She nods as she finishes a bite of salad. "I will get on that but I feel like I need to warn you that it is likely to be a time consuming and costly process. Are you on board with that? I assume you want to be sure to do it all the right way, no cut corners?"

"Very much. No cut corners period. Everything needs to be far aboveboard and I want it to be nice. You take your fees and know I will be fine. My husband died a hoarder of money and was unable to take a cent with him. I only found out recently when we cleaned out his office. Do this right, no money worries. You and I are, I think, on the same wavelength. We should be able to happily work together for years to come." I look around to see that the outdoor area where we are seated is empty except for a member of the waitstaff cleaning up so I lower my voice, "especially if my suspicions about you are correct?"

Maggie looks around and seems very uncomfortable, "I am not sure what you mean?"

Devon stands and walks over to engage the wait-person in conversation, "I mean, I think you are a witch like me." I cause a little bit of air to swirl the table top, briefly lifting then setting things down without messing up the whole table. Maggie looks relieved and creates a small thumbs up in her glass and mine. I go on, "Oh, so glad I wasn't reading you wrong. We should be great working together. And I can be a bit more free in what I tell you. Do you have any prejudices against any of the magical community?"

She shakes her head, "No, honestly I keep it a secret from most people that I married a wolf. His family is good with it and so is mine, it's the general magical public that isn't always okay with these things."

I nod, "Yes, my sister had a flare up over Devon but she sorted herself out pretty quickly."

"Oh?" she glances over her shoulder at Devon, "Hm, vampire?"

I nod and she says with a smile, "He does well, I wouldn't have guessed had we not started discussing it.

My Dario hides his shifter ability too, as does his uncle Benjamin."

My eyes pop. "I had no idea. I've known Benjamin for years, and I would not have pegged him for a shifter. That explains so much about the meeting earlier. He seemed very protective and between him and Devon I felt like I had brought a set of bodyguards with me. It was all very amusing, the property manager whom I will forever call sir dickbag," Maggie giggles at the nickname, "thought he was going to seduce me and get me to sign some crap contract. The two of them bristled up and bulldozed him. I think I was there for snark and legalities."

Maggie nods, "That sounds like uncle. I guess sir dickbag should just be glad they didn't eat him."

Salads finished we push away our plates, "So you will get together with your uncle and go through these properties and call me if you have any issues?"

"Yes. I don't think there will be any issues though. Uncle is pretty thorough and I love what I do. My husband runs a moving company and he does all my heavy lifting. He employs wolves only because it is much easier than trying to hide everything from a regular person. His employees are really loyal even when they aren't family, just because of being part of the magical community makes jobs where you don't have to hide a rare thing."

"Hmm, maybe we can do something about that? Create a company that employs the magical community. I need to think about this, because I have never run a company before. I don't even know what kind of company I could start. Maybe I could fund someone starting a company. Oooh, or just hire someone to do the majority of the things for the company and stay on the board or something? Ugh, sorry, my mind is running down a rabbit's warren of ideas here."

"No problem, I think you could end up doing some really great work. If you need people with ideas or just people for hire, let me know. I know a lot of the magical community. I'm surprised that I haven't met you before now."

I look away, "Well, as ashamed as I am to say it I married a human that was wildly against my using any magic. So I haven't really been a part of the community in a very long time."

"Oh honey, we all do it. Fall for the wrong guy that is."

"I can't even really say I fell for him. I didn't care." I look over to Devon, he smiles encouragingly at me, "I didn't know it then but I was only half here because my mate hadn't found me yet." Maggie looks over at Devon, "Oh, I see. Well no wonder. So this is not your first go round even? Have you done a spell to see how many times you have been here?"

"Well, sort of." Maggie draws her brows down and frowns, "Someone tried to mug me recently. I hit my head when he grabbed me and it knocked loose all these memories."

Her eyes wide Maggie says, "That is crazy. How are

you coping with that? Doesn't your brain feel overstuffed or something?"

"No, it was really jumbled at first but then it settled down and I can go in there and access the memories as needed. It makes sense though, I mean vampires are most often regular humans that are turned. They live hundreds to thousands of years and are able to remember most of it."

"Hmm, I hadn't thought about it like that. You're right. What a great thing to have access to, every memory from every life you have ever lived."

Devon walks over then, "Excuse me ladies, the restaurant says they need to finish setting up for the dinner crowd. I have put them off for a while but we should get going anyway. I took the liberty of paying for the meal."

"Oh, I didn't realize it had been that long!" I stand and collect my purse, Maggie looks at her phone as she stands, "Dario has called multiple times, I need to get back to him before he starts tearing the city apart looking for me. I will get in touch with you as soon as we have sorted some things out. Does uncle have your address?"

"Yes, I am at Devon's place until we decide it is ours or buy another one. Wait, Devon, we need a new house-keeper don't we?"

"Yes, why?" He looks at Maggie, "Do you know of a good housekeeper?"

"I know of quite a few in the magical community that would be great for the position."

His brows raise, "Well that would be great. You have

Fate's number, please do put some in touch so that we can interview them. Mine quit this morning because Fate made coffee for herself." He rolls his eyes and I can't help but laugh, "Ok, Maggie, I will look for calls from you and from your people. I am so glad your uncle suggested you."

"Thank you Fate, I will let him know. I plan to see him for dinner tonight. For now, have a great evening I need to go call Dario." She hustles out of the building with her phone pressed to her ear. I would worry but she is all smiles when he answers. She really just did not want him to worry. I slip my arm through Devon's and we stroll out much slower.

20

Wednesday night arrives and I am heading back to work. With all the projects I seem to be acquiring and the huge amount of money I fell into I think I may need to stop working at the library. I don't know if there are enough hours in the day for me to get it all done properly. I think I will talk to Natasha tonight. I know she will support me one hundred percent and maybe I can lure her away from the library. Hmm, I like that idea.

I make it to the library, the trip is much faster now that I have quit visiting Charlie's grave. I just don't really feel like I want to mourn him anymore knowing what I know now. With all this going on, I really don't have time anyway. Devon and I have been reacquainting ourselves and that process is time consuming but so important for people bonded to each other like we are. I have all the properties that have to be dealt with and they are a whole other level of problem. I didn't know it was possible to feel this level of disgust for a dead man.

I get out of my car at the library, it almost looks foreign to me. I definitely need to quit working here. I walk in and head straight for Natasha's office, tapping lightly I wait for her answer and open the door, peeking around I ask, "Got a minute?"

"Sure, come on in." I step in and shut the door behind me. A few steps more and I sit down in one of the chairs in front of her desk, "I need to talk to you. I feel like I have a lot of projects coming at me and since I fell into all that money, well, I can do those things. I need to give my two weeks notice. And I would like to hire you as well."

Natasha's jaw drops but she recovers quickly, "Ok. I expected the first part, I am actually going through the applicant pool right now. The second part, wow. I mean, what are you planning for me? Are you starting a business? A collective? What do you have planned so far? What is your budget?"

"Well, let me see if I can get all your questions answered. I don't really have a plan just yet, I have the beginnings of one and I want to heavily involve the magical community. Something where we don't have to hide quite so much. Did you know there is a moving company that is run by wolves? They hire only wolves so that they don't have to hide. I want to do more for our community. So, that is as far as I have gotten with that. My budget is quite expansive. I can easily afford to start and continue paying you more than the library is without touching the bulk of my money."

"How much did he have tucked away? Shit girl, you know I get 100k annually from this place, right?"

"Yeah, I know. I have a few hundred thousand in my little account. We found multiple hundred millions and a lot of income property. So… want to come work for me?"

Eyes bugged and jaw dropped Natasha sits there staring for long moments. I begin to wonder if she is ok when she snaps out of it and says, "Let me write up both our resignation letters and get them turned in. You are serious, right?"

"I am. And I don't want to give a whole two weeks, but I will finish this week so you can hire my replacement."

"Girl, we can walk out tonight if you want."

I laugh, "Let's not leave the library hanging like that. You turn in however much notice you want, you have a job as soon as you are ready. Well, now that's settled, I am going to go do some work tonight. Start saying good-bye to the library and to the staff." She nods as I leave, ignoring me in favor of busily typing up resignation letters.

I am so excited, this is going to be a whole new chapter in our lives and we have the resources to make it the best one so far. There is a bounce in my step as I walk over to begin checking in books. I have nearly filled a cart when I see creepy Charles standing in front of my little section of desk. "Can I help you?" I ask like he is a complete stranger in hopes that he will go along with it. No such luck.

"Fate, darling, I have been so concerned for you! Where have you been? No one here would tell me anything regardless of how close we are, or the ring I gave you to cement our promise. It doesn't matter now though. Here you are, fine as ever. You must come have lunch with me. I simply won't take no for an answer."

My jaw is hanging open by the time he gets to the end of his little speech. "You are insane. I have told you without mincing words that I am not interested in you. Not in any way. Ever. You are absolutely insane and I am not under any obligation to fix you. I will not be having lunch or anything else with you. I specifically stated that I would not be bound by your ring. We are not a thing. We will never be a thing. GO AWAY."

Charles' face becomes dangerously red as I speak, but my anger with his shit knows no bounds. He waits till I finish and says, "You should reconsider your position. You are meant to be mine and you WILL BE MINE."

I hear Natasha walk out of her office and come to stand next to me as he continues on, "I will not hear another word of this nonsense. I demand that you take your lunch now and come away with me. I have an entire meal being delivered, we will have a lovely time if you will just stop with this pretense of you not wanting me. How ridiculous."

I look over at Natasha, she seems just as floored as I am by this. We are going to end up exposing our abilities because we have this idiot here unable to comprehend that he doesn't own me. I see her eyes move as she does a mental count of people watching, I look around myself and see that most of the people in the library have come to see what is going on.

That is way too many people. "Charles, you're making a scene. Look around. You are embarrassing yourself with this display. I am giving you one last chance to save face and go do your research. Or we can call security and have you put out. Your choice." People are creeping closer to hear the exchange, Goddess I hope Charles is not a dramatic ass. Natasha's fire is rising to the surface, I can feel the heat coming off of her.

Charles is staring intently at me so I look pointedly at each of the people watching us, about the fifteenth person or so he notices all the people around us. Charles walks off through the crowd, silent but looking that much more dangerous for his silence. I let go of a breath I didn't realize I was holding and Natasha does the same next to me. I can feel the temperature going down and I turn to her, "Go finish calming down. I can disperse the crowd."

She nods, walking off slowly and with the utmost attention to the placement of her feet back to her office. I walk closer to the desk and announce to those still watching, "I think we are done here for the night people. Thanks for being there and witnessing what was going on. Let's all get back to our work now, eh?" People nod or wave as they head back to their seats.

A few come over to ask if I am really ok so I reassure

them. I am so embarrassed that he made such a scene, it doesn't even matter that it isn't my fault. I know how people think, maybe not these people, but people in general. Ugh. I don't know what to do with this kind of garbage. Maybe it is just my own anxieties pecking at me and no one is at all blaming me. I mean, it isn't the dark ages.

21

I go on with checking books in and loading the carts. Stretching I realize it is getting close to time for Devon to get here. I haven't seen Charles leave but he could have walked right past and I missed him. He is probably gone already, he usually is by this time.

I look around, leaning out over the desk but I don't see him hanging around. I decide I can go ahead and start putting the books away, but just in case he is still back there I will stick near the front of the library. No dark corners for me tonight. This library has shelves all over the place, plus displays. I can avoid the back for hours. I wander out to the far side of the open area in front of the desk with my cart of books.

The rhythm of shelving is comforting. It takes a bit more focus to make sure I don't head for the back of the library. I find a stack in the cart that need to be on the display up front. Someone must have checked them out and devoured them. I steer the cart up there and begin arranging the books.

I will miss this part of my job, but I am super excited to start this new chapter in my life. I feel, for the first time in my entire life, like I am whole. My life was so gray without my fated mate that I didn't even realize that it was lacking in color.

A hand grabs my arm in a vice grip and pulls me off my feet and out the doors so fast I don't have time to shout. I remember I am magic, I don't have to take this shit. I solidify a bar of air at knee height to trip this fuckhead.

Too late I realize, he is still holding my arm and we both go down. I manage to cushion my landing, only a second or so before the pavement met with my face. I don't even want to know what hitting my head again would knock loose this time. I lift my head and turn it to see Charles laying stunned on the pavement. Good. Then Devon lands on him and the two are fists and knees and fangs everywhere.

I try to get up only to be smooshed by them rolling over me. I look right and see them rolling down the hill. I kind of enjoy the site because those two are heavy. Footsteps near my ear and a voice saying, "Miss, are you all right? Do you need some help? Those great lumps are too heavy to be rolling over a delicate flower like you."

He has this sweet Irish lilt that is almost hypnotizing and I accept the offer of help up because there appear to be a lot of sore places on me right now. I roll a little to the right and extend my hand to this lovely voice, he lifts me from the ground like I weigh nothing, nearly snatching my arm out of the socket in the process. "OW."

He looks surprised for moment and I watch as realization dawns upon him. "Oh damn, I am so sorry miss! Are you ok? How's your arm? Is it still attached?" My eyes pop a bit at the last question, "Yes, it's there so far. How many arms have you ripped off like that?" I ask as I rub my shoulder a bit to make sure it is still firmly seated in its socket.

He laughs at me, "It only happened the one time Fate. You are Fate, aren't you?" I nod, "Yes, I am. I am also still having to make a concentrated effort to pull up those memories from past lives and I assume you are one of Devon's vampire friends, so if you could just introduce yourself, that'd be great." I look down the hill to where Devon and Charles are still rolling around like teenagers only more bite-y.

He looks at me like I may be a new specimen of bug and feeling it I look back, narrowing my eyes. Still looking at my new comer I reach out with the hand that has been rubbing my shoulder all this time and manipulate the air around Devon and Charles, lifting them into the air and separating the two.

They are still trying to get at each other so I move them close enough that they could almost touch. The dark man standing next to me begins to laugh long and loud, "Oh, you are definitely Fate. I am Billy. Billy Webb. Somewhere in those memories of yours you met me and we were great friends because you have this beautifully twisted sense of humor. And it looks like that is soul deep."

He turns serious, "You know, you probably should go ahead and separate them. You know who the one that isn't Devon is, right?" I nod, "Of course. That is Creepy Charles," I tell him as I move the two further apart, "also known as the guy that has been stalking me and who just tried to kidnap me. The schmuck!" I rotate my first finger in Charles' general direction flipping him over so he hangs upside down midair. Billy snorts, controls himself and tells me, "I'm sure he is all those things. But he is also Devon's sire. And the man that keeps killing you."

All the air in my lungs is gone. Gasping, I try to process this, nearly falling but Billy grabs me with those strong arms of his, gentle this time. I finally gasp some air into my lungs and croak, "That's— That's him? Creepy Charles is the guy that keeps killing me?" Billy rubs my back pretty vigorously, "Yeah. Guess you didn't know that. Sorry, I would have broke it to you differently if I had realized."

A full breath of air in my lungs now I straighten up though Billy keeps a hand on my arm. I turn to look at the two men hanging in the air. Both have stopped struggling and are watching me. I wave a hand and tell the wind to take Charles to Raleigh and drop him there. I watch him fly away fighting the wind. It won't do him any good. I let Devon down gently and he runs to me, "Are you ok? I am so sorry, I went into a rage when I saw him dragging you along the sidewalk. I've never seen him trip before though, was that you?"

"Yeah, I tripped his punk ass. I also told the wind to drop him in Raleigh. I did not specify from what height. Devon, that is Creepy Charles."

All the color drains from Devon's face, "That is who has been stalking you?" He crushes me in his arms, "Oh God Fate, I could have lost you again. I had no idea. My sense of smell is not great, my face was broken and I lost it before I was turned. I had no idea he was around. He has always been able to block me from sensing him. He's been here every night, oh god."

"Uuhdslfsuulalhbklf."

Devon loosens his grip, "What was that love?"

"I said I can't breathe! You're suffocating me!" He lets go and I take a few deep breaths, Billy leans in, "You know, it is really strange that he has been this close and you still breathe. What has he been doing? Why is he Creepy Charles to you?"

I give him a short rundown of what Charles has been doing, I happen to catch the two men exchanging a look, "Speak up or hang in the air. I got no more patience left in me tonight." Billy laughs while Devon scowls. Growing serious again Billy tells me, "It would appear that either Charles has decide that stealing you would be a more fitting punishment for Devon or he is in actually love with you. I don't know which is more dangerous."

22

The wind carried me all the way to Raleigh before it dropped me in the middle of a back alley from about two stories high. She's a witch in this life too I see. I pick myself up, the suit is ruined. Someone will pay for the insult. Rubbing my hands together I dust off the worst of the grit. My phone fell out somewhere.

I walk the streets looking for a good human target. There. She looks similar enough to Fate that I can pretend I am feasting on her sweet blood, turning her and marking her as my property. I follow the woman, leaving plenty of space between us so as not to make her nervous.

She is holding her phone to her ear, pretending to talk to someone. She must have sensed I am following her. Prey usually does sense the predator in some way. I wait till she is walking past an alley to make my move.

Putting on the speed I run up and grab her, jumping into the alley. Before she can scream my lips are clamped to her sweet neck, fangs buried in her flesh.

She doesn't taste as sweet as Fate's witch blood but her blood slakes my thirst and her death my need to kill for tonight's insult. I stop long before she is dead, licking the wounds to close them. One quick twist and her neck snaps. I drop her to the ground. Humans are so fragile, the least little thing kills them. I walk back out of the alley and pick up her phone. It is an old flip phone, I hate them. So old and out of style.

This is what you have reduced me to tonight Fate. I look forward to punishing you well for your misbehavior. Though, now that I think about it, it is a good sign that she sent me here instead of having the wind tear me apart. I feel certain she has enough command of the wind to do so and it wasn't as if she could have been worried about witnesses with as long as she left us hanging in the air next to the library.

Yes, very encouraging. She loves me and as soon as I rid the world of Devon we can be together. With that bond she can't do anything but be with him, whether she loves him or not. She must have fallen in love with me over these past weeks but Devon being there is preventing her from acting on her feelings.

Dialing a number I hit the call button. My lackey answers, "Who the fuck is this?"

"It's me."

"Oh shit. Boss, I had no idea, this ain't your number.

Why you calling from a strange number? Something happen to your phone?"

I roll my eyes, stupid humans. "Yes. Something happened to my phone. I need a ride. Come to Raleigh, pick me up at the..." I look around, see a sign for a place called Caffe Bellezza, "Caffe Bellezza."

"Where's that at boss?"

I roll my eyes again, "Google it fool. Be here within the hour or suffer the consequences." Hanging up the phone I step in to the café. I order a creamy café latte with a double shot. The staff is quick but they annoy me with their stares at my clothes. If I hadn't fed recently I would wait for them to finish here. I take my latte over to a nearby bench and sit to wait for my ride.

23

My last night at the library, I am so relieved. I haven't seen Charles since the night I sent him flying to Raleigh but Devon and Billy have been with me everywhere. In fact, Billy is at the desk now flirting with Natasha. It is adorable watching the two of them spar. She says he is annoying and he says she is equally annoying.

I wonder how long it will take them to notice that they have been flirting since they met? I shelve the last few books in my cart and push it toward the desk. I run a hand across Devon's shoulders as I walk by and giggle when he shivers. He smacks my butt before I get out of reach. I turn and shake my finger at him, making a face. He laughs and I delight in the sound. He is so serious so much, all this worry about when and where Charles will pop up again because we know he will return.

I get it, but I suppose I am a little more at peace with

the idea because I know I will be back and my Devon will find me if Charles manages to kill me again. But then I think about how I felt after Charlie died and I don't blame him. I wouldn't want to go through that again either.

I open the drop door and step behind the desk, "Billy, go bother Devon. We have our paperwork to fill out so we can leave. Then you can walk her to her car for," I make the air quotes sign, "safety." The two of them glare at me and I laugh as I shoo Billy away. Hooking my arm through Natasha's I lead her back to her office. "That man is insufferable, Fate. I don't understand how it is possible that Devon is friends with him."

"Mmhmm. Yes indeed."

"I will set you on fire. Don't try me. He has been annoying me all night and now you want him to walk me to my car!"

"It really is for safety. Charles could be out there and use you to get to me and Devon. I need you safe. Billy is older and stronger than Charles, that is part of the reason why he is here. Strength in numbers and all that jazz. Come on, get that paperwork out so we can be done here. I want to go home and get some sleep before we give all that up to create a whole business."

"All right. But that man really is insufferable."

I try not to smirk as she prints out the paperwork for our last nights' work here at the library. I look around the office and remember all the times we hid in here to talk because we couldn't talk about things at my house and

Charlie didn't want me wandering off places after work. Probably he was worried I would catch him with one of his looks-like-me women. "You know, while we are sitting here doing paperwork you could tell me about that look from the other night."

Natasha looks over at me confused so I remind her about the night we got drunk and I told them about Devon being a vampire. "Oh! That! Yes, I knew Devon was a vampire. I knew Charles was a vampire. I know about Anelle and her boyfriend as well as all the random people around here that are part of the magical community. I forget that most people don't see these things immediately. I found a really old spell in my family grimoire that allows me to see each person as they are, to know them for what they may be. It has kept me pretty safe and taught me that we aren't all that different. People are people, no matter what else they are beyond a regular person."

"Oh, no way? I know that is a family spell, but would you care to share it or at least cast it on me? I feel like that would be really useful as we move into this new venture."

Natasha stops what she is doing, "Yeah it would, I see what you mean. I need to check with Mama first, but I think she would be fine with it."

"While you check with her about that, I have another thing to ask you. I was chosen a long time ago to preserve witch lore. If she is okay with it, I would love to preserve that spell as well as any others your family might be willing to share."

Natasha's mouth shuts with an audible click of her teeth, "Girl. Is there anything else you haven't told me yet?"

"I am thinking about becoming a vampire?"

"Oh? Well, that's whatever. I meant something important."

"Nah, that pretty well covers it. There are more details but you have the big notes now."

THIRTY MINUTES and a mound of papers later we leave the office for the last time. Devon and Billy are waiting for us near the door. I snuggle up under Devon's arm as we leave the library one last time. On the way to the car I see a woman that looks so similar to me it can't be an accident. Especially since she is heading right for me and looks mad as hell.

She stops in front of us and starts screeching at me about Charlie and a house and things owed. Something in me snaps and I step right up to her, "Shut your screech hole. It's not bad enough my husband cheated on me with you, now you want to come harass me as I go about my business? Woman, I will take an assault charge. I have bail money, how bout you?"

Her jaw hangs open, I suppose she is shocked because I would have taken this back when Charlie was alive.

"You have two minutes to tell me what you are doing

here in a calm manner or we are gonna discuss that charge now."

She takes a deep breath, "You took all the properties! The money from those was supposed to go to me! That was how he was going to take care of me, I was supposed to be set for life after all the things I did for him."

I shake my head. I feel a little bad for her, not bad enough to give her those properties or any of the rents from them, but sorry that she was taken in by Charlie. "I hate being the one to break this to you, he never meant for you to have them. He made sure I would inherit, repeatedly checked to be sure."

"NO." This girl is shaking her head at me chicken style, "You were supposed to die and I was going to take your place." She claps a hand over her mouth, realizing what she said and takes off running.

Devon asks, "Want me to catch her and bring her back?"

"No, but I think maybe we need to watch out for a killer that might not care his employer is dead." I scan the parking lot as a chill goes up my spine. Devon hustles me off to the car and we pick up Billy on the way out of the lot.

🐦

AUTHOR'S NOTE

I hope you have enjoyed Fate's story as much as I enjoyed the writing of it. I wrote a novella about her origin story, where she came from long before she ever married Charlie or even Devon. Her journey has been long and it's going to be even longer before she finds some peace.

You can get the novella free for signing up to my monthly newsletter and you can sign up for that on my website rhiannonfutchwriter.com

The Fate's Chronicles series is completed now, the final book released on July 27, 2021. I hope you have enjoyed this book and that you will enjoy the rest of the series as well.

Thank you for reading what the voices in my head told me!

Rhiannon

P.S.

Reviews really help other people decide whether or not to read a book. If you feel a way about this book, I would sincerely appreciate a review.

ABOUT THE AUTHOR

Rhiannon writes steamy paranormal romance. She is an avid reader of many authors in a variety of genre though she tends more toward paranormal.

She has three former pound puppies that she dotes on and three daughters that she adores.

Rhiannon has lived in multiple states though she is currently residing in North Carolina. Wandering, witching, and reading with her puppies and husband are what she does when she isn't writing.

To learn about what is happening in Rhiannon's world and get loads of pupper cuteness, sign up for the by using the QR code below to visit my website.

ALSO BY RHIANNON FUTCH

The Daughter of the Moon series-

<u>Selena Rose, Daughter of the Moon Book 1</u>

<u>Thorns of the Rose, Daughter of the Moon Book 2</u>

<u>Heart of the Rose, Daughter of the Moon Book 3</u>

The Fate's Chronicles series

<u>A Vampire's Fate</u>

<u>A Vampire's Treasure</u>

<u>A Vampire's Dream</u>

<u>A Vampire's Chase</u>

<u>A Vampire's Fight</u>

<u>Fated for Halloween -</u> only available via email signup

The Belancore Witches of North Carolina series

<u>Witchy Ever After</u>

<u>A Witchy New Year</u>

<u>My Witchy Valentine</u>

Sin series

<u>Sin on a Dark Knight</u>

<u>Sin on a Broken Heart</u>

<u>Sin on a Burning Heart</u>

Sin on a Vengeful Heart

The Vampire Kings Series

Mercy of the Vampire King

Shame of the Vampire King

Pursuit of the Vampire King

Prey of the Vampire King

Reign of the Vampire King

Coming Soon

Love and Vampires Series

Olivia's Fall

Olivia's Prison

Olivia's Flight

Olivia's Family

Warriors of the Old Gods

A Dream of Blood

A Dream of Wolves

A Dream of Stone

A Dream of Ravens

A Dream of Bones

www.ingramcontent.com/pod-product-compliance
Lightning Source LLC
Chambersburg PA
CBHW030759190726
48285CB00003B/942